ADVENTURE ISLAND

THE MYSTERY
OF THE HIDDEN GOLD

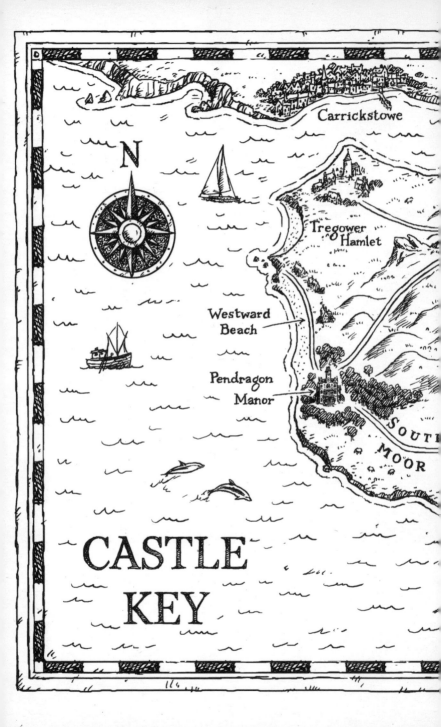

Carrickstowe

N

Tregower
Hamlet

Westward
Beach

Pendragon
Manor

SOUTH
MOOR

CASTLE
KEY

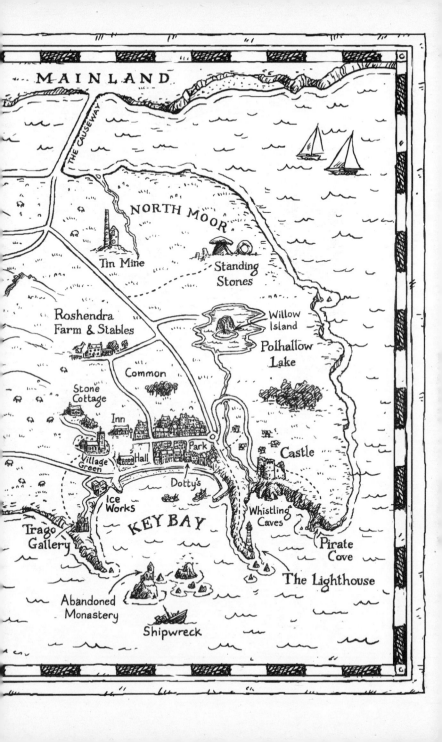

Collect all the Adventure Island *books*

- ☐ The Mystery of the Whistling Caves
- ☐ The Mystery of the Midnight Ghost
- ☑ The Mystery of the Hidden Gold
- ☐ The Mystery of the Missing Masterpiece
- ☐ The Mystery of the Cursed Ruby
- ☐ The Mystery of the Vanishing Skeleton

ADVENTURE ISLAND
THE MYSTERY OF THE
HIDDEN GOLD

Helen Moss

Illustrated by Leo Hartas

Orion
Children's Books

First published in Great Britain in 2011
by Orion Children's Books
a division of the Orion Publishing Group Ltd
Orion House
5 Upper St Martin's Lane
London WC2H 9EA
An Hachette UK company

3 5 7 9 10 8 6 4 2

A catalogue record for this book
is available from the British Library.

ISBN 978 1 4440 0330 7

Printed in Great Britain by
Clays Ltd, St Ives plc

For Jak and Lana

One

The Secret in the Cellar

*N*eed . . . *somewhere . . . to hide . . .*
Jack hurtled down the spiral staircase three steps at a time.

There were some awesome hiding places in The Lighthouse. Emily had squeezed into an old trunk of ropes on the seventh floor. And they'd practically had to call in Search and Rescue to find Scott behind the old clockwork winding mechanism in the lantern room.

OK, Jack had to admit it *was* a good spot, but you'd think his brother had discovered life on Mars, the way he'd been gloating about it ever since. Which was why Jack *had* to find somewhere even better.

He paused on the fifth floor and glanced through the porthole window. A flash of lightning ripped through the swirling black clouds, lighting up the scene like an X-ray. Waves the size of double-decker buses were hurling themselves against the cliffs. The elements – sea, sky, rock, thunder, lightning – were slugging it out in an epic punch-up. And in The Lighthouse, they had ringside seats for the big fight! The breakers were crashing against the walls and the wind was rattling the window-panes. The storm was so violent that Emily's dad had switched on the lamp in the lantern room and the friends had only just made it inside without being swept off the promontory!

But right now Jack had more pressing concerns than the storm. Scott would probably have counted up to fifty already. In fact, knowing Scott, he wouldn't even have bothered to count. He'd just wait a few seconds, before shouting 'ninety-nine, one hundred, coming, ready or not . . . '

Where can I hide?

Jack hurried down the stairs, past the three floors of guest rooms – Emily's parents ran The Lighthouse as a Bed and Breakfast – past the kitchen on the first floor, to the guest lounge on the ground floor. Several of the guests were sitting around reading or playing board games. The storm had knocked out the main power supply, and although it was only late afternoon, the angry storm clouds darkened the sky. Emily's mum and dad had lit candles and the old wood-burning stove. The soft firelight flickered across the colourful rugs, sofas and wall-hangings that filled the huge circular room. The family who were staying at The Lighthouse for the week were playing Ker-plunk. A clatter of tumbling marbles was followed by a scream of *'That's not fair!'* and a squawk of *'He cheated!'* from the six-year-old twins.

Must focus on hiding . . .

The spiral staircase descended one more floor, to a cellar hewn deep into the rock. Jack had already hidden down there once, behind a rack of old lifejackets and oilskins, but it was worth another look. He grabbed a torch from a hook by the front door and headed down.

The cellar was cool. Jack shivered. The earthy scent of damp rock reminded him of the Whistling Caves, where he'd had to swim out underwater to escape the rising tide – not an experience he'd particularly enjoyed! That was not long after he and Scott had first come to stay with Aunt Kate while their dad was digging up bits of old pots in the middle of an African rainforest-slash-war-zone. The brothers had run into Emily Wild on their first day in Castle Key (literally: they were being chased by a stampede of cattle at the time!). Together the three of

11

them had discovered a hoard of stolen Saxon artefacts in the caves, not to mention a secret passage to the castle. Since then, they'd also escaped from a haunted room *and* rescued a runaway film star.

No, this wasn't your *average* kind of summer holiday!

But, then, Castle Key wasn't your *average* kind of island . . .

Jack shone the torch around. The cellar was crammed with a random collection of crates and boxes and trunks. There were cases of wine, a box of canvases for Emily's mum's paintings, a set of golf clubs . . . Some of the stuff looked prehistoric! *Dad could probably get funding for an archaeological dig down here,* Jack thought. *But if I can just shift this ancient crate . . .* The crate was surprisingly heavy. *What's in this thing? Someone's collection of bowling balls and encyclopaedias?* But Jack was on a mission now. He shoved harder. Suddenly it budged.

Time was running out. This would have to do! But as Jack wedged himself behind the crate, he stubbed his toe on something hard. Cursing with pain, he shone his torch down. The culprit was a rusting iron ring. Curious, he gave it a quick tug. From beneath a carpet of dust, a wooden trapdoor creaked up out of the stone floor.

Ker-ching!

Scott and Emily wouldn't find him down *here* in a million years!

'OK, we give up!' Emily shouted. She looked at Scott. 'You don't think he's mad enough to have gone outside to hide, do you?'

'Mad enough?' Scott laughed. 'This is *Jack* we're talking about. Of course he's *mad* enough. He'd go surfing in a tsunami!'

That's what I was afraid of, Emily thought. 'He could have been swept out to sea in the storm . . .' She ran to the front door and pulled it open. 'Jack! Come back!'

'Shut the door!' A chorus of protests came from the lounge as a gale force wind roared through the room like an express train.

'No one has gone outside!' Mum shouted. She was playing Monopoly with one of the guests – a Japanese salesman called Mr Tanaka – and the wind had scattered her money all across the rug.

Emily sighed. *Where is Jack?* Drift – her pet dog, constant companion and partner in numerous investigations – was nudging his head against her knees. His black ear was standing up and his brown-and-white spotted ear flapped up and down. Emily knew he was trying to tell her Jack was in the cellar. She followed him downstairs – even though they'd already searched down there a hundred times. Drift was usually the ultimate sniffer dog, but this time the excitement of the storm must have fried his tracking circuits.

'*You're* going to have to say it!' Emily told Scott, after they'd scoured the cellar yet again.

'Say what?' Scott asked.

'That you give up, of course! Jack doesn't care whether I find him or not. He only wants to beat *you*.'

Scott groaned. Emily was right. But having to concede defeat to his younger brother was about as cool as doing up your top button and tucking your shirt in. Every fibre of his being was screaming, *Don't do it!* He swallowed, cleared his throat and squeezed the words out through clenched teeth. 'OK, I give in. You can come out now!'

'Sorry, didn't quite catch that!'

Scott whipped round. Jack's muffled voice was coming from somewhere close by but where *was* he? Had he found an invisibility cloak or something? 'I give in!' Scott uttered the dreaded words a fraction louder.

'Can I get that in writing?' Jack's grinning face appeared from behind a crate. Cobwebs smothered his spiky blond hair and dust smudged his cheeks like camouflage paint.

'But we looked behind there!' Emily gasped.

'I was down in that hidey-hole.' Jack stretched his arms. 'Phew, it's not exactly five-star accommodation, is it?'

'What hidey-hole?' Emily asked.

'The one under the trapdoor.'

'What trapdoor?'

Jack stared at Emily. 'You mean you didn't know it was there?'

Emily shook her head.

Oh, yes! What a result! Jack did a victory lap of the cellar. This was better than he could have hoped. He'd *only* found a secret hidey-hole that Emily didn't know about, right under her nose!

Together, they dragged the massive crate out of the way.

'Wow!' Emily breathed. 'I had no idea this hole was here . . .' She was about to carry out a full inspection when she noticed a roll of paper in Jack's hand. 'What's that?'

'Dunno! It was just lying on the ground down there.' Jack perched on the edge of a broken table and unfurled the scroll. 'It's got some old writing on . . .'

Emily and Scott pooled the light of their torches on the dog-eared sheet of yellowing paper. It was freckled with brown spots and the ink had faded to the colour of a tea stain.

'It's a letter!' Emily cried. She tucked her tangle of chestnut curls behind her ears and knelt down to examine the faint words. She made out a date at the top of the page: August the fifth, 1902. A shiver of excitement ran down her spine. *The letter was over a hundred years old!*

The three friends peered at the letter.

To Captain John Macy,

During the weeks that you have sheltered me here since you pulled me from the storm-tossed seas, I have come to regard you as a true and loyal friend.

For this reason I will now make known to you a secret of great import. First, I confess I have not told you the full story of the terrible night that The Empress went down in the bay of Castle Key.

On that fateful night, I made my way into a lifeboat, along with my fellow officer, Tommy Spring, and a certain valuable cargo. In the teeth of the storm we found ourselves thrown onto an uninhabited rocky islet. Uncertain of what events lay ahead, we hid the

'Hid the what?' Jack slapped his hands to his forehead. 'He can't just *stop* in the middle of a sentence. That's mental cruelty!'

Emily's dark brown eyes gleamed. 'Ooh, I bet it was *contraband*! Brandy or muskets or something.'

Scott and Jack looked at each other and laughed. 'Smugglers?' they chorused. Emily suspected *everyone* of being a smuggler. If she hadn't already marked them down as being a spy, that was! If the letter had turned out to be a shopping list, she'd have been on the lookout for a rogue grocer dealing in black-market baked beans and Pot Noodles. But, Scott had to admit, there was an outside chance she could actually be right this time.

A shipwreck, a secret of great import and something hidden on a rocky island . . .

They'd been planning to play Cluedo next. But Cluedo could wait.

They had a *real* mystery to solve now.

This letter had Adventure written all over it!

Two

Another Exciting Discovery

'There must be another page somewhere . . . ' Scott said. But he was talking to himself! Jack, Emily and Drift had already piled into the hole.

Drift yelped.

'Sorry, mate,' Jack said. 'Didn't mean to stand on your paw!'

'I can't see a thing with you in the way!' Emily complained.

Scott laughed. 'You guys look as if you're trying to break the Guinness World Record for the most people in a confined space!'

Jack climbed out and gave Emily room to shine the torch around. There didn't seem to be any holes or alcoves built into the rough walls. But Drift didn't let that fool him! The little dog was a medley of many breeds – but his nose was one hundred per cent pure bloodhound. And that finely-tuned nose was picking up something *very* interesting in the back corner.

Emily examined the wall where Drift was scrabbling with his paws. 'Give me your penknife, Jack!' she called. She inserted the small blade into a hairline crack, and twisted. Something gave a little. She levered the blade further and a piece of the wall eased out like a loose brick.

Emily's heart was racing as she reached into the gap. Her fingers brushed against a rectangular object with a smooth surface. 'It's a book!' She hoisted herself out of the hidey-hole and helped Drift clamber out after her. 'You're a canine genius!' she laughed, wrapping her arms around him.

Scott stared at the book in Emily's hands. It was the size of a fat textbook and bound in rusty maroon leather. It was probably an old Bible or a dictionary. He couldn't help feeling disappointed. Antique books might be interesting – if you were into that kind of thing – but it *wasn't* page two of their mystery letter.

But when Emily prised open the stiff pages, they were filled with spidery handwriting. 'It's a journal!' she breathed. She cracked the front cover open. Inscribed on the first time-mottled page were the words, *Property of John Nathaniel Macy, 1902.*

Jack whistled. 'Wow! That's the guy the letter's addressed to.'

There was a long silence. The three friends looked at each other in amazement. *This journal could hold the answers! What was the secret? And what had been hidden on the island?*

—

Bursting with excitement, they settled down in the dining room, where the light was better for reading the journal's faded handwriting. The dining room was housed in a conservatory added on to the side of the lounge – so that the guests could enjoy panoramic ocean views over their breakfasts. At least, they *could* when the windows weren't being lashed by horizontal rain and sea-spray. Luckily they were made of extra-tough reinforced glass. The power was still off so Emily fetched an oil lamp from the dresser. She struck a match, lit the lamp and turned the wick up inside the curved glass mantle so that it cast a pool of bright light across the table.

Emily carefully placed the journal in the middle of the table. She took a deep breath, and was about to open it at page one, when Jack reached out, grabbed the book by the covers and gave it a good shake.

'Hey, what are you doing?' Emily protested.

Jack shook the journal again. A sheet of paper fluttered onto the table. He punched the air. 'Bet you a million pounds it's the missing page!'

Emily stared. Jack was right! The handwriting matched the letter exactly. She lined the two pages up side by side and read the last words of the first page '. . . *we hid the . . .*' and the first word of the second page '. . . *cargo*'.

Jack thumped the table. 'Cargo? *We hid the cargo?* Yeah, that really narrows it down! Why can't this guy just cut to the chase and tell us what it is?'

'Hang on!' Emily said. 'Let's see what else he's got to say.' She continued to read. '. . . *which had come into my possession in the Transvaal . . .*' She hesitated. 'Where's the Transvaal?'

'It's where Count Dracula comes from,' Jack said. An awesome thought suddenly occurred to him. 'Hey, you don't think this guy's a *vampire*, do you? This letter could be written in *blood*!'

Scott rolled his eyes and shook his head slowly. 'That's *Transylvania*, you duh-brain!'

'Anyone know where Transvaal is?' Emily called through to the guest lounge.

'Ooh, is this a quiz?' Mrs Hartley, the mother of the Ker-plunk family, looked up from the game. 'I love quizzes! Now, don't tell me, *Transvaal* . . . I'm sure that's South Africa.' There was a mighty crash. 'Now, which one of you two knocked the game over?'

'He did!' the twins chorused.

Emily grinned. 'Remind you of anyone?' she asked.

Scott and Jack looked at each other blankly and shook their heads.

Emily laughed. Then they all leaned forward to continue reading.

We then returned to the lifeboat and rowed for the shore, planning to return at a later date to recover our property. The storm raged on and our little boat foundered on the treacherous rocks. Tommy was washed overboard, the Lord have mercy on his soul, but I was saved by your good self and brought back to the lighthouse. Lately, I have heard that men have arrived in the village asking of my whereabouts. They have followed me from Africa in search of the cargo, which they claim I stole from them, although who is to deny a soldier the spoils of war? But I must flee and lie low until they cease to search for me here.

I know you will not double-cross me, so in case any accident should befall me, I leave you this map for safekeeping. If I do not return within three months, you may use it as you will. Do not reveal its contents to anyone for it shows the location of the African gold.

I remain your grateful friend,

William Maddox

'*African gold?*' Scott murmured.

'Now we're talking,' Jack laughed. 'That's my kind of cargo!'

'And there's a map!' Emily's heart was doing back-flips. She could sense mystery and adventure in the air. She flicked through the crackly pages of the journal. *It has to be here.* At last she found it: a sheet of thick parchment stuck inside the back cover. She smoothed it out on the table. The three friends huddled round, their heads almost touching. The ink was badly faded and speckled, but the outline of an island and some scribbled notes were barely visible. The words *Gull Island* were written across the top.

'Gull Island!' Emily cried. 'That's not far. You can see it from here.' She ran to the window and looked west across the bay. Scott and Jack stood behind her and peered out. Thunder rumbled and lightning flashed. A seagull flew past backwards, flapping in vain against the gale-force wind. 'At least, you can *usually* see it . . .' Emily sighed.

'Anyone in here hungry?'

Jack turned to see Emily's mum entering the dining room. She was in one of her long paint-spattered kaftans, her wild black hair pinned up with a pair of pencils. More importantly, as far as Jack was concerned, she was carrying a tray of toast and hot chocolate she'd made on the wood stove in the lounge. Hungry? He was *ravenous*!

Jack sank his teeth into a piece of buttery toast and

sighed happily. *Could this day get any better?* He was in a lighthouse, in the middle of a storm, poring over a century-old treasure map by the light of a flickering oil lamp. He was a pirate on the high seas, searching for a chest of gold doubloons buried on a desert island. OK, so pirates probably didn't snack on toast and marmite, and they probably didn't have Emily's dad – aka Seth Wild, the ex-guitarist of a famous eighties rock band – strumming Bon Jovi's *Livin' on a Prayer* in the background. Maybe he should put in a request for *Yo Ho Ho and a Bottle of Rum . . . .*

'What was that?' Scott asked.

'Er, nothing, just clearing my throat,' Jack mumbled.

'So you *didn't* just say "yo ho ho"?' Scott teased. 'I must have imagined it.'

Emily giggled.

'So, where's the X?' Jack asked, quickly changing the subject. 'Any decent treasure map *must* have an *X marks the spot.*'

'And you're a leading expert on treasure maps, are you, Captain Jack Sparrow?' Scott laughed. Although, he'd secretly been scanning the map for an X too. There wasn't one. Instead, there were arrows and numbers and some notes scrawled in the margins. 'I get the feeling William Maddox didn't want to make this map too easy to figure out in case it fell into the wrong hands. What d'you think, Em?'

But Emily was only half listening. She was lost in

John Macy's journal. She'd found the entry for the night *The Empress* went down in the storm. Macy's words told how the lantern in the lighthouse failed during a ferocious tempest and *The Empress* ran aground on the dangerous reefs in Castle Key Bay. John Macy described how he rowed out and rescued a lone survivor. 'Listen to this,' she told the boys. '*William Maddox is most insistent that I not inform another living soul of his survival . . . and since he is so weak after his ordeal in the storm, I have agreed to his request, but I am resolved to discover the reasons for his secrecy when he is stronger. I suspect there may be foul play . . .* '

'Yeah, he's nicked some gold in Africa and buried it! That's pretty foul!' Scott said. 'What about August the fifth – the date of William Maddox's letter?'

Emily turned the pages. 'Here it is. Yes, he says he's surprised to find that Maddox has left without warning. Then there's a bit about finding the map and the letter. He says he's going to keep them safely hidden but he's wondering whether he should go to the police.' Emily paused. 'Hmm . . . that's weird . . .' she murmured.

Scott shrugged. 'Not really. He must have been an honest citizen.'

'No, not that. *This* . . .' Emily pointed to the journal. 'There're a few more entries. Just routine stuff about the weather and the tides . . . nothing about Maddox turning up again. But then the journal just stops. The last date is August the twentieth, 1902.'

Three

Operation Gold

Scott sighed and raked his fingers through his sun-streaked brown hair. 'We solve one mystery and another one pops up to take its place! We know what Maddox hid on Gull Island. But what happened to John Macy?'

'Maybe Maddox came back and found out Macy was thinking of handing the map over to the police so he bumped him off,' Jack said, miming a gory throat-slitting episode.

Emily nodded. 'That *would* explain why the journal entries just stop . . . '

Suddenly the room was filled with dazzling light. 'Aggh!' Jack clapped his hands over his eyes. 'I'll talk, I'll talk!'

The electricity had come back on.

There was a round of applause from the guest lounge.

Scott looked out of the window. While they'd been engrossed in the journal and the map, the storm had blown over. The waves had calmed to a restless roll. The sky was a clear stained-glass blue. 'Oh, no!' he groaned under his breath. He'd been hoping to be stranded at The Lighthouse for the night. It wasn't that there was anything wrong with Stone Cottage. In fact, Scott had grown to love Aunt Kate's little house on Church Lane – well, apart from the flowery cushions and the teeny-tiny telly, maybe! But he'd always wanted to spend a night in The Lighthouse, and when Emily's parents said it was too dangerous to walk back along the promontory to the village in the storm, he and Jack had leapt at the chance.

'It's OK boys, you can still stay. I've already made up beds for you in the living room upstairs,' Emily's mum said as she came into the dining room and began opening windows. 'It's so stuffy in here. We need to let some fresh air in.'

'So, what are we waiting for?' Jack asked, as soon as Mrs Wild had gone. 'Let's go bag us some African gold!'

Emily laughed and shook her head. 'It's a long way to

row to Gull Island. And it could take us ages to find it. We'll need a full day and a properly planned expedition.'

Ah yes, planning! Jack thought. *I should have known!* Emily made planning into an art form. She couldn't even open a packet of crisps without figuring out the optimum strategy.

Emily fetched her notebook from her bedroom. She turned to a new page, wrote *Operation Gold* and underlined it three times in red pen.

A balloon of excitement inflated in Jack's chest. This was their third investigation together, and it could be the biggest and best one yet!

'We'll need to work out what all these scribbled notes on the map mean,' Scott said. 'Maddox hasn't marked the actual location of the gold. We can't just pitch up on the island and start digging random holes.'

Jack shrugged. Actually, that pretty much summed up what he'd had in mind. 'So what do you suggest, O Great and Wise One?'

'Well, since you ask so *nicely*,' Scott said, 'there's an arrow pointing to this little inlet here. I'm guessing that's where Maddox's lifeboat got washed up. And all these notes must be instructions for finding the gold.'

Emily grinned. 'You're right. But they're not exactly obvious, are they?' she said, and began to read out loud. *'Point nose to nearest of the two towers and with both in alignment and with S on the shark . . . '*

'What towers?' Jack asked warily. *Alignment? S?*

This was starting to sound suspiciously like one of those maths problems they were always having to do at school: *if two lines are at right angles to a circle and x = y, what's the square root of infinity?* His brain was hurting already.

'They're like the weird clues in those crosswords Aunt Kate does,' Scott said.

Jack thought crosswords were even worse than maths problems. But to his great relief, Emily jumped up and ran to the window. 'Look, there's Gull Island. You can just see it further out in the bay now the sun's out.'

Jack looked over her shoulder. 'That little white island, you mean?'

'Yeah, its Cornish name is Gwencarrick – which means White Rock.'

'Wow, is that white stuff snow?' Jack asked.

'Snow?' Scott snorted. 'In Cornwall? In August?'

'Think about it,' Emily told him. 'There's nothing there but a gazillion gulls and guillemots and kittiwakes. Let's just say there are no indoor toilet facilities . . . '

Jack had no idea what a kittiwake or a guillemot was but he got the general picture. 'You've kind of spoilt it for me now.'

'That's why the only people who ever go there are birdwatchers,' Emily said.

'And the odd dodgy shipwrecked sailor hiding stashes of gold!' Scott pointed out.

Emily sat back down and studied the map again. 'Two

towers? What towers can you see from Gull Island?'

'The Lighthouse?' Jack suggested. 'Oh, and you could see the castle on the cliff behind us. That's got a tower.'

'Good thinking!' Emily wrote in her notebook. *Clue One: Line up towers – lighthouse and castle?*

'The next bit looks like some kind of code,' Scott said, poring over the map, '*F6-Z4-B3 . . .* '

They were interrupted by Emily's dad entering the dining room carrying a tray of water jugs and tablecloths. 'Sorry to break up the party, kids, but I have to set up for dinner. What's this? A treasure hunt?'

'Oh, yeah, sort of.' Emily quickly tucked the map and journal out of sight. She never *lied* to her parents, but she preferred to keep her investigations under their radar, in case they worried or, even worse, tried to help or something. And it wasn't difficult; Mum and Dad were so busy running the Bed and Breakfast, their radar would hardly even beep if she took up lion-taming in the living room.

Dad ran his hands over his long greying hair and tightened his ponytail. He always did that when he was worried.

'What's the matter?' Emily asked, hoping Drift hadn't been caught sneaking into the kitchen again.

Dad sighed. 'Oh, I was just hoping Simon didn't get caught up in that storm. He went off to Carrickstowe this morning to hire a sailing boat.'

Simon Fox was a guest at The Lighthouse. He'd checked

in a couple of days ago. He was Australian and said he was spending the week in Cornwall by himself to 'get his head straight' after breaking up with his girlfriend. And so far, at least, Emily hadn't established any major holes in his story. *Unlike Mr Tanaka,* she thought, glancing through to the guest lounge. He *said* he was a salesman from Tokyo, visiting a fudge factory outside Truro, but his movements were highly suspicious. There'd been late-night phone calls *and* he'd snapped the top of his laptop down *very* sharply when Emily had tried to catch a glimpse of the screen earlier . . .

'Look! Here he is now!' Jack said.

As if on cue, Simon Fox breezed through the front door. He was tall and broad-shouldered with messy blond hair and blue eyes. Dressed in a faded rugby shirt and baggy shorts, he looked exactly how Emily imagined Jack would look if you fast-forwarded twenty years. He acted pretty much the same way too: like a friendly overgrown puppy. 'G'day all! Bit of a shocker out there!' he said, addressing everyone in the guest lounge.

'You didn't try sailing in that weather, did you?' Dad asked.

'Nah, mate! I'd have given it a go but they wouldn't let me take the boat. I had to entertain myself in Carrickstowe all day. Good thing I like a challenge, eh?'

Everyone laughed.

'Hey, Hiroki, how's tricks?' Simon high-fived with Mr Tanaka.

Emily stared at Simon Fox. *Hiroki?* How had he got to be on first-name terms with Mr Tanaka? Mr Tanaka looked like the kind of guy who'd find the use of his *initial* a bit over-familiar. But Simon's friendly manner was infectious. The Hartley twins stopped squabbling and swung from his arms. Mrs Hartley made a space for him on the sofa. And as for Mum, if she batted her eyelids any more as she offered him a gin and tonic, they were going to fall off.

Jack was starting to find this one-man popularity contest a bit over the top, but then Simon Fox pulled an enormous box of chocolates out of his backpack. 'Picked these up for everyone to share while I was in town. Jack, do you want to do the honours and open them?'

All-round good bloke, Jack thought, as he helped himself to a caramel truffle. In fact, the only one who didn't seem that impressed with Simon Fox was Drift, who curled up on a sofa and ignored him. Probably just annoyed because he wasn't allowed a chocolate. 'Sorry, Drifty,' Jack said. 'Chocolate's poisonous for dogs. Your species has got a major design flaw there.'

Drift flicked his ears. He didn't look amused.

Four

The Investigation Begins

Emily peered at her alarm clock. It was five a.m. but she was wide awake. She'd had a brainwave! A way of figuring out what had happened to John Macy to bring his journal to such a sudden end. She pulled on her dressing gown. Drift looked up from his position curled up on her bed and pricked up one ear. It was the middle of the night, and he was dreaming about rabbits, but he was Emily's Right Hand Dog and he was on standby for adventure twenty-four-seven. Together they crept downstairs.

Emily pushed open the door to the family living room and flicked on the lights.

There was a chorus of blood-curdling groans.

She'd forgotten the boys were fast asleep on the sofas.

'Aggh!' Jack cried, as Drift launched himself onto his head and began licking his ears. 'I didn't do it!'

'Do what?' Emily laughed.

'I was dreaming that . . . er, well, never mind.' Jack sat up and rubbed his hands through his spiky blond hair. 'Gerroff, Drift!'

'Ooomph!' Scott pulled the duvet over his head and turned over.

Jack watched Emily march across the cosy but cluttered room and sit down at the old roll-top desk where her dad kept all his paperwork. She started pulling out folders from the bottom drawer.

'Time to get to work. Investigations don't solve themselves, you know!' she said briskly.

'This one's been waiting a hundred years!' Jack groaned. 'Surely a couple more hours won't hurt. What time is it anyway?'

Emily ignored him. 'These files are all in a muddle. Help me look!'

Jack gave up. When Emily got her teeth into an investigation you might as well try and hold back a tornado with an umbrella. 'Sure,' he sighed, grabbing a bundle of files and rifling through the pages. 'Er, what exactly are we looking *for*?'

'These are all the old records for The Lighthouse. If we can find anything for 1902 we should be able to find out what happened to John Macy – assuming he was the lighthouse keeper. If Maddox did come back and murder him in his bed, there's bound to be a record of it. They must have appointed a new lighthouse keeper, if nothing else!'

Jack started leafing through the records. They weren't exactly a riveting read – page after page rambling on about tide tables and employment contracts and maintenance costs. *Blah . . . blah . . . yawnsville . . .* Jack's eyes were closing when Emily suddenly sprang across the room and landed on the sofa next to him, brandishing a sheaf of papers.

'I've found it! Look! Maddox *didn't* kill John Macy. This is a record of service for John Nathaniel Macy, keeper of Castle Key lighthouse, 1890–1902. *Died in action, during rescue of a stricken fishing vessel, August 21st, 1902.* He was awarded a medal for bravery.'

'That's the day after the last journal entry!' Scott's head popped out from under his duvet like a hibernating tortoise emerging from its shell. He parted the floppy hair curtaining his face and peered through. 'So Macy must have hidden his journal in the hidey-hole before he went out on that rescue mission.'

'I wonder why he bothered hiding it down there,' Jack said.

Emily thought for a moment. 'I was reading through it last night. It was definitely his private journal, not an official logbook for The Lighthouse. Some of the stuff in it was quite *personal* . . . about a young lady in the village he was "courting" . . .'

Jack rolled his eyes. 'Boring! Anything else?'

Emily shook her head. 'Not really, but the point is it was private, full of things that he probably didn't want anyone else to read . . .'

Scott was sitting up now, his grey eyes sparkling with excitement. 'So, if William Maddox never returned, and John Macy died at sea, that means no one has set eyes on that treasure map for over a hundred years!'

Emily bounced on the sofa. 'Which means that the gold is still buried on Gull Island!'

Jack rubbed his hands together. 'And, of course, I should get the biggest share because I found it!'

Scott threw a pillow at him. 'On that argument Drift should get the most. He sniffed out the journal!'

Jack lobbed the pillow back. 'Oh, yeah, what's he going to spend it on? A gold-plated water bowl?'

Drift ran around in circles wagging his tail. He wasn't interested in gold-plated water bowls, but he loved pillow fights!

Jack sprawled back on the sofa. 'So what *shall* we spend it all on? I'm thinking a whopping great mansion – no, make that a *palace* – on a tropical island, with its own BMX track in the grounds and a helicopter pad on the roof . . .'

Scott grinned. 'I'll get a really fast car. And a house with one of those home cinemas and a gaming room kitted out with mega computers and massive screens . . . and a season ticket to Chelsea, of course, and . . .'

'I'd need a private plane and a swimming pool and my own personal pizza chef . . .' Jack was really enjoying himself now. 'Oh, and I'd pay someone to do all my homework for me. But don't worry, I won't let being rich change me in any way.'

'Hello! Earth calling Boys!' Emily laughed. 'We've got to *find* the gold first! We can't be certain Maddox didn't go back for it. And if he stole it in the first place, we'd have to give it back to the original owners anyway.'

'But they'll be well dead by now!' Jack pointed out.

'Their families, then . . .'

'They'll probably give us a *reward* though, won't they?' Jack said, hopefully. 'There might still be enough for just one little mansion between us.'

Emily laughed and started to stuff the files back into the desk. 'Come on, let's get treasure-hunting.'

'I'm hungry,' Jack moaned. 'I can't hunt on an empty stomach.'

Emily glanced at her watch. It was only half past five, but morning sunshine was already pouring in through the windows. 'Let's go to Dotty's for breakfast. They open early for the fishermen. We'll probably find Old Bob in there. We can ask him about Gull Island. I've never rowed out to it before. He'll know what the local currents are like.'

—

Old Bob was sitting in Dotty's Tea Rooms on the seafront with a mug of tea and a bacon sandwich on the red checked tablecloth in front of him. Despite the sunshine, he was wearing his usual woollen hat and thick navy blue jumper and hugging his mug of tea in his gnarled fingers as if he existed in his own personal sub-Arctic micro-climate. The old fisherman looked up from his tea and winked. He'd helped the friends with their investigations more than once over the summer – most recently by providing the getaway boat for the film star Savannah Shaw.

'Heard anything from your Hollywood friend, lately?' he asked, beckoning for them to bring their trays of bacon and eggs over to his table and join him.

'Yes,' Emily replied. She'd received a postcard from Savannah only a few days before. 'She and Max are white-water rafting in Canada.'

Old Bob shook his head. 'Ah, rather them than me. I had enough white water yesterday. Force ten winds out there, it was!'

'Actually, that's what we wanted to talk to you about: a storm.' Emily looked around to check that no one was listening. Luckily the rest of the early customers had taken their drinks outside to sit under the parasols at the pavement tables. The only other person in the café was Dotty, who was busy cleaning the cappuccino machine behind the counter, while singing along to Beyonce's *If I Were a Boy* on her iPod. 'Only this storm was in 1902!' Emily added.

'Ah, right!' Old Bob said without any sign of surprise. '1902. That's going back a bit, even for me.'

Emily explained about the letter from William Maddox and the map of Gull Island.

'Gull Island, you say? Not fit for anything but birds, that place. The rocks round there will cut a boat up something rotten if you're not careful. And there are some nasty rip-tides. But your chap must have drifted quite a way in that lifeboat of his. *The Empress* sank some ways south of Gull Island.'

Old Bob narrowed his twinkling blue eyes and gazed out through the café window towards the sea – as if he could see Gull Island and its treacherous rocks. It seemed he was looking back over the years as well as across the ocean. 'I remember my old grandfather telling me how he saw *The Empress* go down when he was a young lad. Terrible, terrible storm it was that night. The lantern in the lighthouse was struck by lightning. All the villagers went up to the point with their lamps to help warn off the ships, but it was too late for *The Empress*. Transport ship, she was, bringing soldiers back from the Boer War in South Africa.' Old Bob shook his head, lost in thought. 'Ah, what a tragedy! All those soldiers. They'd survived the war. They'd even survived the typhoid fever – and that claimed more lives than the fighting. Then they were shipwrecked just a few miles from the shores of home. Every one of them perished that night. Ah, the sea can be a cruel mistress.'

'*Everyone* perished?' Emily asked, catching Scott and Jack's eyes.

'That's what I've always been told,' Old Bob said. 'I'd never heard of this Maddox fellow . . .'

'Now, I'm not one for ear-wigging and tittle-tattle, of course, but . . .'

Emily, Scott, Jack and Old Bob all whipped round to see where the voice had come from. But the café was empty and Dotty was still singing *If I Were a Boy*.

Then a stooped old lady stepped out from the storeroom at the back of the café, a scrubbing brush in one hand and a bottle of disinfectant in the other.

'Bob Trevithick, you know as well as I do that there were *certain rumours* that the lighthouse keeper had rescued a survivor . . .'

Five

A Long Line of Busybodies

'Mrs Loveday!' Scott almost choked on his Coke. 'We didn't know you were there!'

'Oh, don't mind little old me, dear. I'm just cleaning out the freezers for Dotty.'

Perhaps that explained her outfit; Mrs Loveday was wearing her cycling helmet and pulling off oven gloves and a ski jacket. Although it didn't explain the trainers. They'd clearly been designed for a target market of seven-year-old ballet dancers, rather than seventy-year-old cleaning ladies; the laces were pink and glittery and lights flashed on the heels with every step. Nor did it help Scott get his head round Mrs Loveday's comment. Yes, she had a black belt in Advanced Gossiping, but surely even Mrs Loveday's scandal detectors couldn't pick up events that had happened over a *century* ago!

They all stared at her. Old Bob chuckled and rubbed his chin. 'Irene Loveday, we may be old, but we're not *that* old! *Rumours*? What are you rabbiting on about?'

Mrs Loveday ignored him, pulled up a chair and gave the teapot a hopeful swirl. Emily took the hint and fetched her a cup. The old lady settled herself like a hen on a nesting box. 'I couldn't help hearing you kids asking about the wreck of *The Empress*. Now, my old granny used to tell a story about that night. She wasn't one for idle chitter-chatter, of course . . . '

Jack snorted and pretended it was a sneeze.

'Of course,' Scott murmured. He was having trouble keeping a straight face too. It seemed Mrs Loveday came from a long line of busybodies.

Mrs Loveday smiled at him. Scott had been her favourite 'nice young man' ever since he'd carried a box of paper towels from her bike trailer to the Castle Museum during Operation Treasure. Well, *technically*, Jack had carried the box, but Scott had been more than happy to take the credit.

'Well, Granny heard from Maud Jenkins at the fish

shop that Sally Nancarrow had seen the lighthouse keeper – John Macy, his name was – carrying a man from his boat up to the lighthouse in the dead of night!'

Emily topped up Mrs Loveday's tea. 'And did your granny find out what happened to him?'

'No. Well, that John Macy was a bit of a Dark Horse by all accounts. There was some sort of *carrying on* with the vicar's daughter, but that's another story. All I know is that he kept this mystery man Under Rats at the lighthouse . . . '

'Under *wraps*, you mean?' Scott asked.

'That's right, dear. *Under wraps.* You know, all hush-hush.' Mrs Loveday tapped the side of her nose. 'And he was never seen again, although Granny *did* say that men came to the island asking questions about survivors a few weeks later. *Foreigners*, they were . . . '

'From Africa?' Emily asked, excitedly.

Mrs Loveday nodded. 'Yes, Africans. But not black ones. *White Africans!*' She made it sound as if they were some rare species of wild animal, like snow leopards or giant pandas. Mrs Loveday slurped the last of her tea and picked up her scrubbing brush. 'Well, I can't sit around chattering all day. There's work to do.' Her beady eyes flicked to the café door, which was swinging open. 'Ooh, now, there's that lovely young man who's staying at The Lighthouse, Simon Wolf!'

'Simon *Fox*,' Emily said.

'*Yoo hoo! Simon!*' Mrs Loveday called. 'Over here!'

Simon Fox turned and smiled. 'G'day Irene! Hi Bob! Hi kids!'

Irene? Scott was impressed! Simon had only been in Castle Key a couple of days and he was Mrs Loveday's new best friend already!

'Such a nice young man!' Mrs Loveday said. 'Bought me a cup of tea *and* a Bakewell tart when we were in here sheltering from that storm yesterday. It's so rare to find young people who make time to talk to Senile Citizens these days . . . '

'*Senior* citizens, would that be, Irene?' Simon corrected kindly. Scott was even more impressed. Simon had actually managed to keep a straight face.

Jack was less successful. He had to resort to a full-blown coughing fit to prevent an explosion of laughter. Mrs Loveday glared at him as if he were a hoodie-wearing, graffiti-daubing, litter-scattering example of all that was wrong with the Youth of Today.

Jack glared back. He had no idea why Mrs Loveday had taken such a dislike to him from their first meeting, but he was starting to take it personally.

'Anyone like to help me out with this bacon sandwich?' Simon asked. 'Dotty's given me way too much.'

Jack grinned. 'I'm your man! Bring it on!'

Mrs Loveday tutted. 'Manners!'

Simon winked at Jack and handed him a plate.

Emily had to go to a family party with her parents that afternoon, and Jack and Scott were kept busy for the rest of the day too; an old ash tree in the garden at Stone Cottage had come down during the storm, and Aunt Kate asked them to chop it into logs she could use on the fire.

At dinner that evening Scott couldn't stop thinking about the map. From what Mrs Loveday had heard from her granny, William Maddox had either fled from the White Africans or been killed by them. That meant the gold was still squirrelled away somewhere on Gull Island – with only kittiwakes and guillemots for company. All they had to do was crack those clues on the map to figure out exactly where to search. 'F6-Z4-B3 . . . ' he muttered for the hundredth time. 'It's still not making any sense.'

Jack shrugged. He was excited about finding the gold too, but right now there was chicken casserole on the table and he'd caught a glimpse of a lemon meringue pie in the fridge. 'Some sort of code, I expect . . . '

'Are you boys trying to figure out a secret code?' Aunt Kate asked, peering at them over her glasses as she served casserole and mashed potatoes onto Jack's plate. 'What fun!'

Jack glanced at Scott. Aunt Kate was so wrapped up in writing her soppy romantic novels that, as long as they came home for dinner and didn't get arrested, she didn't generally take much notice of what they were up to. Which was exactly how it should be, as far as Jack was concerned. Adults should be kept in the loop on a purely need-to-know basis. 'Yeah,' he said vaguely, 'it's just this treasure hunt we're doing with Emily . . . '

'F6-Z4-B3, you say?' Aunt Kate patted her hair – which fluffed up like a halo of white candy-floss. 'Hmmm, a sequence of alphanumerical pairs. Probably a simple substitution code. You'll need to find the key, of course.'

'The key?' Scott asked.

'The decoder,' Aunt Kate explained. 'It tells you the relationship between the letters in the coded text and the original message. For example, you might reverse the alphabet and use Z for A, and Y for B and so on.'

Jack gawped at Aunt Kate. *Alphanumerical pairs, substitution code, decoder . . .* where did she get this stuff? 'She must have got it from all those spy thrillers she's into,' he whispered to Scott, as Aunt Kate was taking the lemon meringue out of the fridge. 'I noticed the latest Dirk Hazard one has appeared on the bookshelf.'

Scott laughed, 'And I think she's joined his fan club too. The Dirk Hazard website was open on her computer the other day.'

Aunt Kate placed the pie on the table. It smelled like heaven and the meringue was thicker than a fifteen-tog duvet.

Suddenly Jack forgot all about codes!

Scott took a last spoonful of meringue and leaned back in his chair with a contented, tired-but-happy feeling. The day hadn't started out that well – Emily switching on the lights and Drift jumping on his head at the crack of dawn wasn't exactly his ideal wake-up call – but hacking up a tree with a hulking great axe had turned out to be much more fun than he'd expected, even though his arms were starting to feel as if they'd been run over by steamrollers.

And – best of all – they had another amazing mystery to solve! He pictured himself throwing open the lid of a huge wooden chest full of gleaming gold bars . . .

Tomorrow, he vowed, *I'm going to study the treasure map in detail and copy out the rest of the code. I'm sure I can crack it. In fact, maybe I'll take one of those Dirk Hazard novels to read in bed to get in the zone!*

Six

Officially Missing

Emily would much rather have spent the afternoon chopping firewood with the boys than in Truro with the gathered clans of the Wild family at her Great Aunt Beryl's ninetieth birthday party! It was bad enough that she had to wear a dress and leave Drift at home by himself. Even worse, she was stuck at a table with her three cousins and they had only one topic of conversation between them. It wasn't that Emily had anything *against* horses – they were perfectly nice animals – but after two hours of snaffle bridles, stable fees and Pony Club, she was losing the will to live. She couldn't wait to get home and put in some work on the treasure map. She needed to figure out exactly where Maddox's lifeboat had landed on Gull Island and chart a route so they could navigate to the same spot. In her little rowing boat, *Gemini*, they should be able to pick a way through the rocks.

When at last they got back to The Lighthouse, Emily was pole-axed by one of Drift's vertical take-off welcomes. He sprang into her arms and attempted to bark, lick her face and chase his tail at the same time. Emily picked herself up off the floor and hugged him. 'I've been gone three hours, not three years!' she laughed. 'Come on, we've got work to do!' Together they ran up the spiral staircase to the family living room, where Emily had left the map with John Macy's journal on Dad's desk.

At least, that was where she *thought* she'd left it.

The journal was still there, tucked out of sight behind the computer.

But the map had gone!

Emily's heart went into free-fall. *Think! Think!* she screamed at herself. *Where can it be?* She replayed the scene in her mind . . . she was sitting at the desk, Mum was downstairs shouting for her to hurry up. 'We'll be late for Aunt Beryl's party! *Rápido!*' When Mum started speaking Spanish, Emily knew it wasn't time for a calm and rational exchange of opinions, so she'd quickly stuffed the map and the journal behind the computer and flown down the stairs . . .

But she had *definitely* left the map on the desk.

And it had *definitely* disappeared.

'Mum!' she yelled. 'Did you move anything of mine from Dad's desk?'

'You think I have time for tidying your things?' Mum shouted up from the kitchen, where she was stamping around like a flamenco dancer, crashing pots and pans as she started to prepare the evening meal. She and Dad had been conducting a monster row all the way home in the car about something someone had said at the party.

Dad crept into the living room, clearly looking for somewhere to lie low until hostilities had died down. Mum's temper was just like the storms in the bay – quick to flare up, but just as quick to blow over.

'Have you seen that map I was looking at?' Emily asked.

'Map? What map?' Dad mumbled, without looking up from strumming on his guitar.

Where is it? Emily felt as if she were being sucked down a giant plughole. *Why, oh why didn't I copy the map into my notebook? Why didn't I take it upstairs and lock it in my Evidence Safe?* Furious with herself, she began yanking open drawers and slamming them shut, snatching up piles of papers and banging them down again, and crawling round on the floor to look under the furniture. Drift joined in enthusiastically, grabbing objects in his jaws, shaking them and tossing them aside.

'Er, have you two lost a lottery ticket or something?' Dad asked.

Emily shook her head. This was much, much worse than losing a lottery ticket.

—

How am I going to tell Scott and Jack I've lost the map? The thought chased itself round and round Emily's head all night. She was the one who was always going on about organization and planning being vital for a successful investigation. At one point her overwrought brain hatched the brilliant idea of recreating a copy of the map from memory and passing it off as the original. The boys would never know if she scuffed it up a bit to make it look old . . . well, it *seemed* like a brilliant idea for about five seconds, until she realized that she couldn't remember the details of the coastline or half the coded clues. *F6-Z4, what came next?* The letters and numbers kept jumbling together like alphabetti spaghetti in her head. Why had her memory picked this moment to let her down?

—

'Yeah, right!' Scott grinned at Jack across the breakfast table next morning and pointed at his mobile phone. 'Em says she's lost the treasure map!'

'As if!' Jack snorted into his orange juice. 'Knowing Emily, it's locked in some high-security vault with fingerprint readers and eyeball scanners on the door!'

But Scott's grin suddenly faded. 'I think she's serious . . . ' He held the phone out for Jack to hear. Was that Emily *crying*? No way! Emily didn't *do* crying. The only time Jack had ever seen her in tears before was when she'd dropped a priceless Saxon sword in the sea and thought it was lost for ever – which was fair enough. He'd probably have had a bit of a sniffle himself under the circumstances.

—

Within minutes, the boys were racing to help Emily search. They scoured every inch of The Lighthouse. But it was no good. Their treasure map was officially missing.

Seven

Motive and Opportunity

Scott, Jack and Emily flopped down in Emily's room on the top floor of The Lighthouse in a miserable silence. Drift padded from one to the other, licking their knees to try to cheer them up.

Jack stared at a poster from an Agent Diamond film attached to the curved wall. Maya Diamond, aka their friend, the actress Savannah Shaw, was gazing out across a night-time cityscape, about to abseil down the side of a skyscraper. *I bet Maya Diamond would never lose a treasure map*, he thought crossly. *Especially one that her friend had so brilliantly found in the first place.* 'Well, this is an epic fail!' he grumbled.

'Thanks for pointing that out, Einstein.' Scott's voice was spiked with sarcasm. 'We might not have noticed without your searing insight!'

'All right!' Jack snapped. 'I was really looking forward to finding that gold. And I suppose my private plane's gone right out of the window now.'

'Oh, boo hoo!' Scott mocked.

Emily couldn't bear it any longer. 'WILL YOU TWO JUST SHUT UP?' she yelled, jumping up from her bed and standing in the middle of her room, her pointed chin jutting out and her clenched fists planted on her hips.

Scott and Jack stared. They'd never seen Emily totally lose her temper before.

'Well excuse me for *breathing*!' Jack shouted. He leapt up and stood nose-to-nose with Emily. 'It's your fault, anyway! You're the one who left the map lying around!'

If this turns into a fight, Scott thought, *I'd have to put my money on Emily.* True, she was half the size of Jack, but she was as tough as a terrier and that look in her eye was pure red-mist fury. It was *almost* worth leaving them to it, just to see his annoying little brother being pulverized by a girl! But then he noticed Drift. The poor little guy was cowering behind the bed with his ears quivering, terrified by the prospect of Emily and Jack flattening each other. Scott stepped between them and made a T with his hands. 'OK! Time out! This isn't getting us anywhere.'

Emily and Jack glowered at him. For a moment Scott thought they were both going to turn on him instead. 'The map has obviously been stolen,' he said, in the super-calm voice police negotiators use to talk to armed lunatics. 'We just need to figure out who knew about the map and who could have taken it. Come on, Em, this is basic stuff – motive and opportunity. We've got an investigation to work on – just not the same one we started with . . .' He handed Emily her notebook and her pen, holding them at arm's length as if she might bite his hand off. 'Right, make a new heading: Operation Map Thief.'

Slowly Emily unclenched her fists. She sat down and smiled weakly. Like a firework, her rage had fizzled out as fast as it had flared up. She didn't usually go in for being a drama queen – she left that to Mum and her Artistic Temperament. And Scott was right. They had to find out who had stolen the map – and they had to work fast, otherwise the thief could find the gold first. She took the notebook and pen and sat down. 'OK, who are our suspects?'

'All the guests for a start,' Scott said, breathing a sigh of relief. 'Any one of them in the lounge could have heard us talking about the map when we were in the dining room.'

Emily wrote *List Of Suspects* in the notebook and underlined it. 'Mr Tanaka's my prime suspect. He's almost certainly some kind of spy . . .'

'Or it could be those Hartley twins,' Jack said, his clash with Emily already forgotten. 'They're little monsters. I bet they pinched the map for a laugh.'

'Yeah, I wouldn't put it past them,' Emily agreed. 'They were winding Drift up this morning, teasing him with bacon rinds.'

'And then there's Simon Fox,' Jack said, 'although he seems like a genuine kind of guy.'

'No, it can't have been Simon,' Scott put in. 'He wasn't even *there.* Remember how Mr Wild was fretting about Simon being out in the storm? By the time he came back, we'd put the map away.'

Jack grinned. 'How could we forget? That box of chocolates was awesome!'

Emily chewed her pen. 'The only other time we've talked about the map in public was when we told Old Bob about it at Dotty's. We can rule Old Bob out. I'd trust him with my life! And I'm sure Dotty wasn't ear-wigging. She was too busy doing her own personal Beyonce karaoke routine.'

'Which just leaves Mrs Loveday,' Jack said. 'I *bet* it was her.'

Emily smiled. In Jack's book, Mrs Loveday was

probably responsible for global warming and world poverty as well as the theft of the map. 'I'm sure Mrs Loveday hasn't been in The Lighthouse since yesterday.'

'She could have used black magic!' Jack grumbled. 'I'm sure she's a witch. Wherever we go, she magically pops out of the woodwork, ready to swoop on me for doing *something* wrong. She's worse than a teacher!'

Emily laughed. 'Let's focus on our main suspects first. Ruling out Mrs Loveday and some kind of remote-control witchcraft for the moment, that means Mr Tanaka and the Hartleys. Drift and I will tail Mr T, and you two take the Hartleys.'

Jack groaned. 'Following a couple of six-year-olds around all day: splashing in the paddling pool, making sandcastles, going on the baby swings. Not exactly going to be thrill-a-minute, is it?'

'It's not mean to be *fun*,' Scott said. 'It's a *surveillance* operation.'

Emily nodded seriously. 'Until we find that map we stick to the suspects like superglue.'

Jack grinned. 'OK, I'm in! Just call me Mr Sticky! *No one* is getting their hands on that gold and cheating me out of my private plane!'

⌒

Next morning Jack was woken by Scott's mobile phone playing a Kaiser Chiefs track on the other side of the small slope-roofed bedroom they shared in Stone Cottage. Scott pulled the blankets over his head and grunted, so Jack reached groggily for the phone and peered at the screen. It was a text from Emily.

Hartley family movements now confirmed. Planet Adventure. Hiring bikes from Castle Key Cabin. Leaving t+10.

Planet Adventure. Wasn't that the brand new theme park that had just opened outside Carrickstowe? Jack had been longing to go ever since he'd seen it advertised in the paper. They had this fantastic ride called the Obliterator and a massive House of Horrors. Maybe stalking the Hartley crew wasn't going to be so bad after all!

He leapt out of bed and crash-landed on top of Scott. 'We're going to Planet Adventure!'

'Oomph!' Scott groaned.

'It's our instructions from the Spy Master. The Hartleys are on the move!'

Scott grunted.

'What does t+10 mean?' Jack asked.

'Ten minutes from now. Why?'

'That's when they're setting off. Which means we have to ... *SCRAMBLE*!'

Eight

Trouble in Planet Adventure

Scott and Jack grabbed their bikes from the garden shed and pedalled off down Church Lane as if they were in contention for the Yellow Jersey in the Tour de France. They skidded to a halt on the seafront and ducked down behind the harbour wall. The Castle Key Cabin – next door to Dotty's Tea Rooms – was a classic seaside shop, bedecked with rainbow-coloured buckets and spades and flip-flops and beach towels. They also hired out pedal-boats and bikes. To Scott's relief, the Hartleys were still there, picking out bikes from the racks along the front of the shop.

'We'll take two tandems,' Mr Hartley was saying. Tall, with faded red hair and beard, he was kitted out as if the three-mile bike-ride to Carrickstowe was a solo crossing of the Sahara Desert: hiking boots, those zip-off techno-shorts where even the pockets have pockets, and a backpack bristling with survival gadgets.

The twins were identical, with angelic blond curls and matching scowls on their chubby round faces. 'No way!' the one with the SpongeBob SquarePants t-shirt howled. 'I'm NOT going on a stupid tandem. And that's final, final, FINAL!'

Their dad shook his head. 'You two can't ride on the roads by yourselves. One of you can go with Mum and one with me.'

'You can't MAKE us!' The other twin – who was in full Spider-Man costume – kicked his dad's shin. 'I want *this* one!' He tried to climb onto an adult's mountain bike.

'Now, now, poppet,' Mrs Hartley sighed. 'If you're good boys, Mummy will buy you some sweeties to eat on the way.'

SpongeBob stuck out his bottom lip. 'It'd better be a *jumbo* pack . . .'

Spider-Man dropped the mountain bike. 'Yeah, *and* a Cornetto!'

Behind the wall, Jack shook his head in disbelief. 'We were never *that* revolting, were we?' he whispered. 'They make Horrid Henry look like an *angel*!'

Scott grinned. 'You were *worse*! In fact, why am I saying *were*? You still are!'

—

At last the Hartley expedition was wobbling north on the road towards the narrow causeway that connected Castle Key island to the mainland. Scott and Jack followed at a discreet distance. It wasn't difficult to keep up – especially as Jack's replacement wheel had now been installed on his BMX bile and he was no longer saddled with the Iron Age spare bike he'd had to use to ride to Pendragon Manor during Operation Lost Star. SpongeBob and Spider-Man entertained themselves by throwing toffees at pedestrians and trying to unseat each other from their bikes, as if they were in a medieval jousting tournament. And of course, neither of them pedalled – except when their parents turned round to check on them. Progress was not exactly supersonic!

When they finally arrived at Planet Adventure over an hour later, Jack was hot, fed up and faint with hunger; there'd barely been time to throw on shorts and t-shirts, let alone eat breakfast or make a packed lunch when they left Stone Cottage. But once they were in the queue to buy their entrance tickets, he began to perk up. The intoxicating theme-park soundtrack of screams and clatters and snatches of high-voltage music filled his ears, and the scents of hot dogs and candy-floss wafted into his nostrils. He rubbed his hands together. 'Let's get a pizza and then go straight to the Obliterator.'

Scott put his hands up. 'Whoah! We're here on an undercover surveillance mission, remember. We've got to stick with that lot and find out whether they've nicked our map.' He tipped his head towards the Hartley family, who were queuing two booths away. SpongeBob and Spider-Man were rolling around on the floor, wrestling over a balloon they'd pinched from a toddler's buggy.

Jack groaned. 'But they'll have to go on all the *baby* rides! And it's not like they're rushing off to dig up the gold while they're here, is it?'

'But they might *say* something about it,' Scott explained. 'If the parents took the map, they'll be making plans. If it was the kids, they'll be squabbling over who gets the biggest share of the gold. So just keep your ears open and snoop like crazy; imagine you're Mrs Loveday!'

Jack grimaced. 'Now that,' he said, 'is above and beyond the call of duty!'

Luckily, the family's first stop was the doughnut stand, so Jack and Scott were able to stave off immediate starvation. But after that, things went rapidly downhill.

The Hartleys went on Mini-Kart-Mania, the Woodland Choo Choo and the Little Rascal Pirate Adventure. The boys trudged round after them. Scott had to agree with Jack: it was sheer torture. While they were trundling along on rides with 'mild thrills' they could hear the delicious screams of unbridled terror from the Obliterator. Passengers staggered off, wobbly-kneed, green-faced and giggling.

It was no consolation that the twins felt the same way. '*Why* won't you let us go on the Obliterator?' Spider-Man whined for the thousandth time. 'It's not fair!'

Their Dad sighed. 'Because you're too small!'

SpongeBob stood on tiptoes. 'No we're not! Ben's Dad at school lets him go on the Obliterator all the time. You're *mean . . .*'

Suddenly Scott had a brainwave. 'Let's take it in turns. One of us can stick with the Terrible Twosome and the other can go on the Obliterator. Then we'll swap.'

Jack stared at Scott, filled with a tidal wave of pure adoration for his big brother. If they hadn't been in full view of the carousel, he could have almost hugged him. 'I'll go first!' he said, sprinting off to join the queue.

Scott turned back to the Hartleys. They were having yet another fight about where they were going next. Dad consulted his map of Planet Adventure. 'Next stop, Pets' Corner. Let's see, that's at F6. This way!'

Spider-Man snatched the map. 'But I want to go to the House of Horrors!'

Now that, Scott thought, *would be the perfect place for those two . . .*

Mrs Hartley pressed her palms to her temples. 'You're far too young for the House of Horrors, poppet!'

Scott looked down at his own copy of the map. It was divided into a grid, marked with letters along the bottom and numbers up the side. *F6*, Scott repeated to himself. *That's just like the code on the treasure map. So maybe F6 and the other pairs on Maddox's map are co-ordinates.* But that didn't make sense; Maddox hadn't divided his map into a grid . . .

Suddenly Scott realized the Hartleys were on the move. He spotted them in the crowd and hurried after them. He was starting to think this was a huge waste of time; neither the parents nor the twins had said anything remotely connected with maps, gold or treasure islands. He was considering giving up and heading for the Obliterator when he noticed SpongeBob and Spider-Man peeling off from behind their parents. Mr and Mrs Hartley carried on walking, unaware that their little darlings had given them the slip. For a moment, Scott was paralysed by indecision. Should he run after the parents and tell them? Or should he follow the twins and see what they were up to? If only he hadn't let Jack go off on his own!

He caught sight of a flash of red-and-blue Spider-man outfit ducking under a barrier and made up his mind. The twins were heading straight into the House of

Horrors. Scott elbowed through the queue and vaulted over the barrier after them.

It was dark inside. A flash of sickly green light suddenly lit up an enormous Grim Reaper in a flowing black cloak. Scott saw the silhouette of the two boys standing on the safety rails round a high viewing platform. They were shoving each other and arguing – as usual. 'Call this *scary*?' SpongeBob grumbled. 'It's *pathetic*!'

Scott ran up the steps and looked down over the railing. There was a dizzying drop to the floor below, where a terrified-looking dummy was being attacked by a horde of axe-wielding zombies.

'Get out of my way, dork-brain!' Spider-Man yelled at his brother. Then he clambered onto the top rail and tried to grab the Grim Reaper's scythe as it swung past.

Scott had to do something, even if it meant blowing his cover. 'Come down from there. You'll fall!' he shouted.

Spider-Man turned and stuck his tongue out. 'Oh, yeah! You gonna make me?' He lunged for the Grim Reaper. There was a squeak of trainer on metal as he slipped and pitched over the rail. There were screams from people standing nearby and those looking up from below. But somehow Spider-Man had got hold of a handful of the Reaper's black cloak. He was now dangling by one arm, with nothing beneath him but a long, long drop onto the zombies' axes.

There was a ripping sound as the cloak began to give way.

Scott leapt over the rail. Hanging on with one hand, he reached out and grabbed Spider-Man's shirt. With a superhuman surge of strength, he swung Spider-Man back over the rail onto the platform – and only just managed to stop himself losing his balance and sky-diving onto the zombie display.

—

It took Scott some time to find his way out of the House of Horrors and reunite Spider-Man with his parents. When he finally emerged into daylight, he was dazzled by camera flashes. News of his heroic exploits had clearly spread fast. A jostling crowd mobbed him like seagulls swooping on an abandoned sandwich.

A reporter shoved a microphone in his face. 'How does it feel to have heroically rescued a child from the jaws of death?' he demanded. 'Can you give us a comment for Radio Cornwall?'

Scott felt an arm around his shoulder. Jack was grinning at him. 'So this is your idea of an *undercover* surveillance operation? You've got a lot to learn, mate!'

Scott laughed. For once his brother had a point!

'The Obliterator was awesome, by the way,' Jack added.

Nine

Emily Wild is in the Building

Meanwhile, Emily was stalking Mr Tanaka.

After texting Scott and Jack to alert them that the Hartleys were on the move, she sat in the guest lounge and pretended to be absorbed in playing Bejewelled on her phone while keeping watch on the suspect, who was finishing his breakfast in the dining room. He was pouring himself a second cup of coffee when his phone rang.

'Ah, yes, hello . . . very well, thank you.' Mr Tanaka paused and nodded a few times. 'Yes, I've tracked down the document we were discussing . . .'

Emily had known it all along! Mr Tanaka had taken the map! She squeezed Drift so tight she almost cut off the circulation to his tail.

Mr Tanaka was still talking quietly into his phone. 'We need to prepare for the next phase of operations. I suggest we meet this morning and arrange a visit to the location for later today. And I'd like to keep this under wraps for now . . .'

Emily ground her teeth. *A visit to the location?* He was planning to go to Gull Island and dig up the gold *today*!

'Yes, I'll be there at eleven o'clock . . . ' Mr Tanaka said.

So will I! Emily thought.

Mr Tanaka picked up his shiny black briefcase and headed out of the dining room. Emily glanced up as if she'd only just noticed he was there. He smiled and brushed imaginary specks of dust from the shoulders of his crisp white shirt. 'Good morning, Emily. Are your parents around? I'd like to order a taxi.'

Emily couldn't help admiring his nerve. How could he speak to her so *normally* when he'd stolen her map? It was probably in his briefcase right now. She'd noticed he never let that out of his sight.

But two can play at that game, she thought. 'I can

72

do that for you, Mr Tanaka,' she said in her politest voice, walking across to the antique table they used as a reception desk. 'If you just let me know the address, I'll phone the taxi company for you.'

Mr Tanaka smiled. 'Certainly. It's a company called West & Mitchell. They're on the Penrose Business Park in Carrickstowe. Can you ask the taxi to come at ten thirty, please?'

Emily nodded and made the call.

At ten fifteen the taxi driver rang through to The Lighthouse reception to confirm that he was waiting to pick up Mr Tanaka at the end of Harbour Road – which was the nearest cars could get to The Lighthouse as there was only a narrow footpath along the promontory itself.

'Your taxi's here!' Emily called. Mr Tanaka was sitting with his briefcase on his lap reading *The Financial Times*. He glanced at his elegant Rolex watch. 'It's a bit early, but never mind. There's never any harm in being punctual, is there?'

Which is exactly what Emily had been hoping he'd say when she ordered the taxi for ten fifteen. It gave her an extra fifteen minutes to cycle into Carrickstowe and find West & Mitchell's offices before Mr Tanaka's meeting started. She should just be able to make it by eleven o'clock! She was going to catch Mr Tanaka red-handed. All she had to do was blag her way into the office building, find a hiding place with a good view of the meeting, and capture Mr Tanaka and his accomplices on camera, poring over the map. She'd borrowed Dad's video camera for the purpose. She then had to get the map back, of course, but she'd worry about that part later.

'Come on, Drift!' she said. 'We've got work to do!'

—

It was almost eleven by the time Emily found the office building, an impressive multi-storey block of sandstone and smoked glass. She leaned her bike against a wall. Drift hopped down from his special custom-built basket on the back and followed her through the revolving doors. They found themselves in a vast lobby gleaming with white marble surfaces. Emily didn't know what West & Mitchell did, but she was pretty sure this *wasn't* the fudge factory Mr Tanaka had claimed he was in Cornwall to visit.

'Can I help you, miss?' A man in a security guard's uniform called out from behind a shiny counter. He looked Emily up and down. She was glad she'd tied her unruly hair up in a plait, and switched her usual t-shirt and frayed denim shorts for the dress she'd been forced to wear to Aunt Beryl's party.

'Er, yes, please.' Emily approached the counter. 'There's a man called Mr Tanaka here for a meeting. He's staying as a guest at my parents' hotel . . .' Emily thought *hotel* sounded swankier than *Bed and Breakfast*,'. . . and he left his credit card on the breakfast table so I've come to return it to him.' Emily held up an envelope containing a small flat object the size and shape of a credit card, but which wouldn't be much use on a shopping spree since it was, in fact, Emily's library card. 'If you tell me which room he's in, I'll run up and give it back . . .' She glanced at the bank of lifts at the back of the foyer.

The security guard rubbed his hand over his shaved head. 'Can't let anyone in the building without a prior appointment.'

'But I'll only be a minute,' Emily wheedled.

'Rules are rules. You leave that card with me and I'll see he gets it.'

'Oh, er, it's OK,' Emily mumbled. 'I suppose I can give it back to him tonight.'

'Yes, I suppose you can! Now, stop wasting my time.' Suddenly, the guard noticed Drift sitting at Emily's side. 'Get that dog out of here. And don't tell me he's a guide dog. I wasn't born yesterday!' And with that, he swept Emily out through the revolving doors and onto the street.

Emily glared at her reflection in a mirrored window. She was simmering with outrage. Mr Tanaka and his shady sidekicks were somewhere inside that building rubbing their hands in glee, plotting to shoot off to Gull Island – no doubt, in some fancy company speedboat – to steal *her* gold. Well, she wasn't going to stand for it!

A white van with Jenkins Janitorial Supplies stencilled on the side buzzed past and disappeared round the side of the building. Janitorial supplies. That meant toilet paper and stuff, didn't it? Maybe there was another way in! Emily called Drift and sprinted round to the back of the building. The van had pulled up in a parking bay outside a set of double doors marked DELIVERIES.

The driver got out and pulled open the back doors of the van. Whistling the James Bond theme tune, he folded down a ramp, wheeled out a large trolley of supplies and headed into the building. 'Yes, this is it!' Emily whispered to Drift. But then she noticed something: there was a CCTV camera on the wall pointing directly at those double doors. If she tried to sneak in, the security guard would be after her in a flash.

She glanced back at the van. Mr Jenkins-Janitorial had left the doors open and there was another trolley inside. She checked the angle of the camera. There was no way it could see the van. She had an idea! Admittedly, it was a *crazy* idea – the kind *Jack* would come up with – but time was running out. She had to do *something* . . .

Emily sprinted to the van. The trolley was basically a cupboard on wheels, with sliding doors to hide the contents. Heart pounding, she hauled out three boxes of toilet cleaner and a vat of liquid soap and hid them under a coat in the corner of the van. Then she climbed inside the trolley, bundled Drift in with her and slid the doors shut.

Moments later the trolley jolted into life. Emily held on tight to Drift and closed her eyes. They were thrown to one end as the trolley tipped down the ramp. Then there was a long stretch of trundling and juddering and veering round corners. Eventually they rattled to a halt. Emily strained her ears and heard doors opening and closing. She knew she had to get out fast before Mr Jenkins-Janitorial reached into the trolley for his toilet ducks and found a girl and a dog instead – like a magician pulling a rabbit out of a hat – although she suspected Mr Jenkins wouldn't find it terribly *magical*. She hadn't really thought through the whole getting-out-of-the-trolley-without-being-seen part, she realized, but it was too late now.

Slowly, she slid the door open a crack. The smell of disinfectant hung in the air but all was quiet. She opened it a little further and saw white tiles and a row of wash-basins. She was in the toilets. A door opened and there was the *click clack* of high heels. Emily breathed the biggest sigh of relief she'd ever breathed in her entire life. She was in the *ladies'* toilets! She opened the doors wide, grabbed Drift by the collar and bolted inside a cubicle, just as Mr Jenkins-Janitorial came back into the room.

'I don't *believe* it!' he shouted, rattling the trolley out into the corridor. 'My bloomin' toilet cleaners have walked. People will nick *anything* these days!'

'We did it!' Emily whispered into Drift's fur. *It may*

not have been the most dignified entrance, she thought, *but Emily Wild is in the building!*

When the coast was clear, Emily and Drift sneaked out of the toilets and roamed the maze of corridors. Luckily most of the office doors had a window in them, and she was able to peep in. She saw computers and photocopiers and flipcharts and people sitting around big tables with bottles of water and laptops in front of them.

She was starting to think she'd *never* find Mr Tanaka, when she finally spotted him. He was deep in conversation with two other men and a woman, all dressed in suits, pointing at a map on the table. Her heart in her mouth, Emily was reaching into her bag for the camera when Drift's ears suddenly flicked up. She froze. A voice was speaking into a walkie-talkie somewhere nearby.

'Yes, I've had reports of an intruder ... an unauthorized girl with a dog ...'

Ten:

The Toss of a Coin

I t was the security guard!

Frantically, Emily looked around for somewhere to hide. There was nothing in the corridor but a drinks vending machine set in a small alcove. She squeezed into the gap at the side of the machine and pulled Drift in with her. If they kept very, very still and they were very, very lucky the guard might walk straight past them.

They kept still – even though Drift's fur was tickling Emily's nose – but luck was not on their side. A pair of mirror-polished black boots came to a stop on the carpet tiles in front of the vending machine. The security guard sighed and then there was a jingle of change. *Oh, no, he's going to buy a drink!* Emily heard the coins drop and then a *ker-thunk* as the machine dropped a plastic cup into its dispenser and began squirting in hot coffee. The dispenser was millimetres from Drift's super-sensitive ears and it was a very loud *ker-thunk*. It was too much, even for a dog as highly trained in the art of undercover surveillance as Drift.

He threw back his head and howled.

The game was up!

'I don't know *what* you think you're playing at, young lady,' the security guard boomed, as Emily crawled out from her hiding place. 'But I'm sure the *police* will be able to find out.'

Emily stared at the shiny gold buttons on his jacket, trying to think of something to say – *anything* that wouldn't just dig the hole she was in even deeper. At that moment, the door of the meeting room opened and Mr Tanaka and his three accomplices stepped out into the corridor.

Mr Tanaka raised his eyebrows. 'Hello, Emily. What are you doing here?'

Emily glared at him. This whole mess was entirely his fault!

The security guard tried to hide the look of surprise on his jowly face. 'You *know* this girl?'

Mr Tanaka nodded.

'Well, she *claims* to have something of yours to return!'

Mr Tanaka patted his trouser pockets. 'Oh? I don't *think* I've lost anything . . . '

'Hand it over, Missy!' the guard said triumphantly.

Emily had no choice but to take the envelope out of her bag and hand it to Mr Tanaka. Frowning slightly, he tore it open and held up a blue and white card. The words CARRICKSTOWE LIBRARY SERVICES were clearly printed for all to see.

'If that's a credit card, I'm a performing seal!' the security guard laughed. His hand was already reaching for his phone. No doubt he had the police station on speed-dial.

Emily braced herself for serious trouble.

But to her astonishment, Mr Tanaka smiled. 'Incredible, isn't it? Looks just like an ordinary library card! You'd never know it was really a *credit* card. It's a new security technology that's just coming on-line in Japan. You see, thieves don't bother stealing these because they look worthless.'

'May I?' One of the businessmen standing behind Mr Tanaka took the card and held it up to the light. 'Amazing what they can do these days! I want one of these!'

Emily was dumbstruck. Where was the shouting? Where was the finger-pointing, the handcuffs, the dog-catcher, the *just you wait till your parents hear about this*?

Mr Tanaka turned to Emily. 'Thank you for returning it to me. Clever of you to realize it was valuable.'

'Yes, well, get that dog out of here!' The security guard turned on his heel and stomped off down the corridor.

Emily looked at the carpet. 'I'm sorry,' she mumbled. 'I thought you were a spy.' Funny how something that sounded perfectly sensible when it was in your head could sound so idiotic when you said it out loud.

Mr Tanaka smiled at Emily. 'I realized the other day that you had me under observation. You were quite right to suspect that I'm not a fudge salesman. But neither am I a spy! My company is investing a great deal of money in re-opening the old fish-processing factory in Carrickstowe. It will mean hundreds of new jobs and be a huge boon for industry in Cornwall, but we didn't want the media to hear about it before the deal was complete. That's why I've been tucked away at The Lighthouse rather than at one of the big hotels where I might be recognized. Well, that and the fact that I adore old lighthouses! Anyway, I'm happy to say that we have just finalized the last few details and will be going public this afternoon.'

Emily felt her face burning with shame. She could hardly lift her eyes from the carpet tiles. 'I'm so sorry.

We thought you'd taken a map of ours . . . '

Mr Tanaka smiled and held up his hands. 'Not guilty. Now I must go and prepare for the press conference!' Halfway along the corridor he turned and called back, 'Oh, and by the way, Emily, you might want to call in at the library on your way home and renew your card. It expired six weeks ago!'

—

Next morning, Emily called a meeting with Scott and Jack to compare notes. They met on the rocks above the inlet halfway along the promontory where Emily kept her rowing boat, *Gemini*. It was a place they could talk without being overheard.

Emily pulled out her notebook and turned to Operation Map Thief. 'OK, let's have the full report,' she said, her pen poised over the page.

Jack grinned. 'You mean you've not seen the papers this morning?' He pulled a copy of *The Carrickstowe Times* out of his back pocket and held it up. On the front page was a photo of Scott outside the House of Horrors, looking super-cool with his hands in the pockets of his jeans and his sun-streaked brown hair flopping across his face – although he was wearing a slightly bemused expression. The headline above the picture screamed, TEENAGE HERO SAVES SPIDER-MAN FROM ZOMBIE DEATH PLUNGE.

'The reporters must *love* Scott,' Jack laughed. 'How often do they get a headline like *that*?'

Emily looked at Scott and slowly laid down her pen. 'And this was your idea of *undercover* surveillance?'

Jack clasped his hands and batted his eyelashes at Scott. 'Our *Teenage Hero* couldn't help himself!'

Scott thumped his brother's arm and then recounted the full story. 'But, anyway,' he concluded, 'none of the Hartleys said anything about the treasure map all day. They didn't take it!'

Emily shook her head. 'Nor did Mr Tanaka.' She tucked her knees under her chin and told the boys about her eventful visit to West & Mitchell. 'I feel really bad about suspecting him. Mr Tanaka's the nicest man you could meet!'

Jack grinned. He'd have given anything to be a fly on the wall when Emily was dragged out from behind the vending machine with Drift doing his werewolf impression – although he had to admit, disguising herself as a pack of loo rolls to get inside the building had been a stroke of pure genius! 'So, you didn't exactly stay under the radar either!' he teased.

Emily couldn't help smiling. 'I think you could say we *all* blew it! But at least we've made some progress . . . '

'Oh, yeah, like what?' Scott asked.

'We've eliminated two of the main suspects from our enquiries,' Emily pointed out. She ruled lines through the names in her notebook.

'So now we're down to Mrs Loveday and Dotty?' Scott asked.

Jack gazed out across the harbour and the bay. In the distance, Gull Island sparkled like an iceberg in the morning sun. It was taunting them! 'Why don't we just jump in *Gemini* and head out there now? You never know, we might just find the gold.'

'Spend the day poking around in mountains of bird poo, more likely!' Scott said.

'Exactly!' Emily agreed. 'We'd be better off concentrating on finding the map.'

Yeah, that's what I was afraid of. Wading through bird poo was bad enough but, as far as Jack was concerned, it would be a walk in the park compared to stalking Mrs Loveday.

'I wish we'd solved those clues on the map before it was stolen. Then it *might* have been worth going to look,' Scott said. As he spoke he had a mini-flashback. He was in Planet Adventure listening to the Hartleys squabbling over the map. 'I was thinking about those letter-number codes on the treasure map,' he went on. 'They can't be co-ordinates because I'm sure there was no grid on the map, but I think they're something like that rather than a code . . .'

Emily nodded. 'If Maddox had had a compass with him, he could've given the direction and the number of paces to walk . . . like North-6 or something.'

Jack shook his head. 'Naughty Elephants Squirt Water!'

'What *are* you talking about?' Scott and Emily asked in chorus.

'That's how I remember the compass points: N, E, S, W. But the letters on the map are all, like, F, B, Z and stuff. So that can't have been what Maddox was on about. If he'd just had a satnav with him he could've given us the co-ordinates and made our lives a lot easier!' Jack said.

Emily laughed. 'I don't think they had GPS in 1902! And I don't suppose he had time to pack a supply of handy navigational tools as he escaped from the sinking ship anyway.'

'No, he was too busy loading his treasure chest onto the lifeboat!' Jack pointed out. 'But a heap of gold bars or nuggets wouldn't be much use for finding your way around!'

Scott closed his eyes and tried to think. It was so *frustrating.* Maddox's system had to be simple enough for him to have come up with it at night, in the middle of a storm, without any fancy equipment. So *why* was it so hard to figure out?

Emily sighed. 'Come on, let's go and find Mrs Loveday. We might as well get started.'

Jack scowled. 'No way. I vote we go to Gull Island.'

Scott wasn't in the mood for another showdown between Emily and Jack. The last one had almost ended in mortal combat. 'Let's toss a coin for it!' He pulled a ten-pence piece from his pocket and flipped it.

'Heads!' Emily called.

Scott uncovered the coin on the back of his hand. 'Heads it is. Mrs Loveday, here we come!'

'That's so not fair,' Jack groaned. 'I wanted to call!'

But Scott didn't hear Jack's protests. He was staring down at the coin – at the Queen's profile and the words ELIZABETH II DG REG FD 2008 round the border.

He jumped up and treated Jack and Emily to a triumphant air guitar solo. 'Oh yeah! I think I've cracked it!'

Eleven

Drift's Amazing Magical Nose

Emily and Jack stared at Scott as if he'd lost his mind. Even Drift sat up and twitched his ears uncertainly.

'Maddox used a *coin*!' Scott shouted.

'A coin?' Jack asked. 'What do you mean?'

'One thing we *know* he had with him was the gold, right?' Scott explained. 'Well, if the gold was in the form of *coins,* then he could have used one of them like a compass. He could have used the letters round the edge

89

to record direction. So when it says F6, that means you have to find an F in the writing round the edge of the coin, and then go six paces in that direction . . . .'

Scott sounded so sure, but there was something Jack didn't understand. 'I don't get it. How do you know which way to point the coin in the first place?' He took the coin out of Scott's hand. 'Look! If I hold it this way, the Z in *Elizabeth* is level with the lighthouse. But if I rotate the coin, then it's pointing at Drift's nose!'

Scott was about to tell Jack to engage his brain, when he realized his brother was actually *right* for once. A coin wasn't like a compass – it didn't automatically point to the North Pole. His heart sank; he'd been so sure his coin theory was right.

But suddenly Emily jumped up. 'Oooh, oooh! I know.'

'You sound like a deranged owl, Em!' Jack laughed. 'We're dying of suspense here!'

Emily pulled herself together. 'Drift's nose . . .'

Scott stared at Emily. Yes, Drift's nose was a finely tuned instrument, he'd give her that much, but surely even *Emily* didn't think that Drift's nose had the power to locate magnetic north. The stress of losing the map must finally be getting to her.

Emily grinned. 'When Jack said about the coin pointing to Drift's nose, it reminded me of one of the notes on the treasure map . . . Something about pointing your *nose* so the two towers are aligned. What if Maddox was talking about the nose on the coin?'

Scott looked back down at the ten-pence piece in his hand. 'Yes! That would work. The Queen's nose is just like an arrow!'

'Careful,' Jack laughed. 'It's probably high treason to say things like that.'

'Yes, that's how you line the coin up in the right position!' Emily was jumping up and down on the rocks again. 'Oooh! Oooh!'

'Uh oh! That owl's back,' Jack said. 'Has Drift's Amazing Magical Nose revealed another mystical secret?'

Emily laughed. 'No, but there's something that John Macy says in his journal.' She pulled the journal out of her bag – she hadn't let it out of her sight since the map had been stolen – and flicked through the pages. 'Here it is. I didn't take much notice of this before, but now it makes sense. *This morning Maddox insisted on giving me a gold coin in payment for looking after him,*' she read out. '*He advised me to keep the coin safe as it "may prove more valuable than I know" . . .*'

'Oh, yeah!' Scott high-fived with Emily. 'That *proves* we're on the right track! William Maddox left the coin for Macy to use as a – what was that word Aunt Kate used? – a *decoder* to work out the instructions on the treasure map in case he didn't come back.'

'Just one minor problem with your brilliant theory,' Jack said. He didn't like to let Scott get too big-headed; being a Teenage Hero *and* a Master Code-Breaker was going to make him *unbearable*. 'We've no idea what

91

kind of coin Maddox was using. So we don't know the position of any of the letters, do we? I don't suppose it was a 2008 ten-pence piece. '

But Scott was on a roll. 'We know it was 1902 and Maddox was on his way back from the Boer War. He said his gold was "spoils of war" so it must have belonged to the South Africans they were fighting. With all that information I'm sure the internet will give us some answers.'

Jack grinned. Trawling the internet for South African coins of the early twentieth century didn't exactly sound thrill-a-minute, but it definitely beat trailing around after Mrs Loveday. 'OK, but I could do with an ice cream first. My brain's hurting after all this thinking, and those church bells aren't helping either!' The bells of St Michael's had been pealing out in frenzies of *ding ding DING ding, dong dong DONG dong* for hours. 'It's not even Sunday.'

'No, it's the third Thursday of the month,' Emily said.

Jack stared at her. 'Oh, of course,' he said sarcastically, 'third Thursday of the month is well known as Noisy Religious Music Day all over the world!'

Emily laughed. 'No, just in Castle Key. It's the Bell-ringing Society's practice day.'

Scott got up from the rocks and stretched his legs. 'D'you think we could use your dad's computer, Em? See if we can identify the most likely coins?'

But Emily had gone. She was hurrying along the path in the direction of the village, with Drift trotting along behind her. 'I've got a better idea!' she called over her shoulder. 'We'll go to church!'

Jack looked at Scott and shrugged. 'Are we praying for divine inspiration now?'

Emily laughed. 'You could try. But *I'm* going to see Colin Warnock.'

'The curate?' Jack asked, remembering the friendly guy with the purple Mohican and biker's leathers who'd been playing *Bohemian Rhapsody* on the church organ when he and Scott had met him.

'Yeah, Colin runs the bell-ringing group,' Emily said. 'You thinking of joining?'

Emily laughed and shook her head. 'Colin's also a *collector*. He collects old vinyl records and stamps . . . and *coins*. He gives talks about it. It's dead boring, but . . .'

'But *sometimes*,' Scott laughed, '*dead boring* is just what you need!'

Twelve

Expert Advice

S t Michael's Church was deserted. And silent. The bell-ringers had packed up and gone.

'No problem!' Emily said. 'They always go to the Ship and Anchor for a pint and a pasty afterwards.'

Scott grinned. Did *anything* happen in Castle Key that Emily didn't know about?

Colin Warnock was sitting at a trestle table at the front of the old white-washed pub in the village square. He was wearing a studded leather jacket over a black shirt and white dog collar. The bell-ringers were all laughing as Colin recounted a hilarious story about the church bells in Tregower, the hamlet on the other side of the island.

Scott, Jack and Emily took up position at a nearby table beneath a row of hanging baskets overflowing with pansies and geraniums.

'We're never going to get Colin away from the bell-ringing posse for a private word,' Jack groaned.

Emily smiled. 'Watch and learn!' She arranged her face into an expression of deepest angst and approached Colin's table. She leant over and muttered something to him. 'Mission accomplished,' she said as she sat down again. 'He'll be over in a minute.'

'Wow! What did you tell him?' Scott asked.

Emily grinned. 'Oh, just that there's a gang of girls cyber-bullying a friend of mine at school. He's the village youth counsellor and he loves to help with that kind of thing.'

'Is that even true?' Jack asked.

'Of course,' Emily said. 'Those girls are always at it. It's not a problem though. We set up my friend's account to forward all their messages to the headmaster so *he's* the one they've been telling is "a total loser who'd better watch out"! But Colin will give me some nice sensible advice on standing up to bullies and then Scott can slip in the question about the coin at the end. Here he comes now . . .'

'Cool! He's bringing some Cokes and crisps over for us too!' Jack observed. 'I always liked this guy!'

—

'. . . and if it happens again, Emily, tell your friend she can always come and talk to me about it,' Colin said kindly, draining the last of his pint.

Scot seized his moment. 'Oh, Colin, could I just ask you about something else while you're here?'

'Of course,' Colin said. 'I expect you're missing city life and your friends in London? Finding it hard to adjust to the quiet life of a country bumpkin?'

'Oh, no, nothing like that.' Scott realized with a jolt of surprise that it was true. He hadn't thought about London for ages! And life here was anything but quiet. Beneath its cream-teas-and-sandcastles image there was more going on in Castle Key than on a Saturday night in the West End!

Scott glanced round to make sure no one was listening in. He spotted Simon Fox arrive and sit down at a table not far from the rowdy bell-ringers. Within seconds, he was mobbed by two elderly ladies who seemed to recognize him. Soon they were showing him pictures of their grandchildren. Scott grinned. Poor Simon – he was one of those people that everyone wanted to talk to – especially old ladies! Simon gave Scott a friendly wave and went back to looking at the photographs.

Scott lowered his voice – just in case Mrs Loveday was lurking behind a hanging basket, dusting the pansies. 'I heard you were a bit of a coin expert?'

Colin grinned. 'I dabble, I dabble!'

Scott nodded. He steeled himself to utter possibly the most uncool words he'd ever spoken in his life. He adopted an eager and slightly geekish expression. *All in the line of duty*, he reminded himself. 'I've been getting really interested in coins lately, especially ones from the Boer War period.' *Well, it's true*, Scott thought. As from about half an hour ago, he was *extremely* interested in them!

Colin raised his glass. 'Ah, you're a fellow *numismatist*, are you?'

Scott looked at him blankly.

'A student of coins and currencies?'

'Er, yes, I guess so!' Scott mumbled.

Colin's eyes lit up. Jack recognized that glint. It was the look of an enthusiast who thought he'd found someone as obsessed as he was, and was now going to go off on a three-hour lecture. Time to zone out!

It wasn't quite three hours, but Jack had finished his Coke and crisps – and helped himself to Scott's too – by the time Colin got up and waved goodbye. 'Very interesting talking to you, Scott. I'm off home now so I'll take a photo of that Kruger Pond I was telling you about and pop it round to Stone Cottage for you in an hour or so . . .'

'Er, *Kruger Pond*?' Jack asked, once Colin had left. 'What do we want a picture of some old pond for?'

Scott shook his head. 'You didn't listen to a single word Colin said, did you?'

Jack screwed up his eyes and strained to remember. This was worse than being at school! 'Yeah! It was something about not letting bullies win ...'

Emily laughed. '*Pond* is Afrikaans for *pound*. The Kruger Pond is a gold coin that was around in South Africa in 1902 ... According to Colin, thousands of them were buried in the Transvaal by people fleeing from the war. It's almost certainly the kind of coin Maddox got hold of and brought back with him aboard *The Empress* ...' Emily took out her notebook and wrote down the details, '... and that he buried on Gull Island!'

'And Colin has one in his collection,' Scott added. 'Once he gives us the photo, we'll be able to follow Maddox's directions.'

Jack grinned. 'The Teenage Hero strikes again!'

Emily looked up from her notes and shook her head sadly. 'At least we would be able to if we had the map!'

Thirteen

The Terrible Truth

Emily had to go home and help her mum in the kitchen at lunchtime, but with some high-velocity potato peeling and turbo-charged pastry rolling, she was sitting on her bed, re-reading Macy's journal for any further clues, when the doorbell rang.

'We've got the photo of the coin!' Scott shouted, as he and Jack hurtled up the one hundred and twenty stairs to her room.

Emily placed the print-out on her desk. Colin's photograph showed both sides of the Kruger Pond, one above the other. On the tails side was a coat of arms, but it was the head that Emily was interested in: a serious-looking bearded man staring off into the middle distance.

'That's Paul Kruger,' Scott said. 'He was the president at the time.'

'And just look at that nose,' Jack added. 'Pointing right at our treasure!'

Emily read the words printed around the edge of the coin: *ZUID AFRIKAANSCHE REPUBLIEK.*

'That means South African Republic,' Scott explained.

Jack rolled his eyes. 'I think Em could probably have guessed that!'

Emily couldn't take her eyes off the words. All the letters in the code were there: F, B, Z . . . This had to be the right coin! For a moment she was jubilant. But suddenly her happy bubble popped. Now they'd cracked the code, it just made it even *more* maddening that they didn't have the map with the rest of the information they needed. It was like doing the whole of the sky on a thousand-piece jigsaw and then finding that half the straight edges were missing. To find the right starting position to follow the coin-directions they knew they had to line up the two towers. But there had to be some way of knowing *where* along that line to stand. Otherwise, it would be like knowing the row but not the column in a game of Battleships. That second piece of information had to be in the clues on the map somewhere. On top of that, they could only remember three of the coin directions – F6, Z4 and B3 – but there'd been several more scribbled in the margins of the map.

Emily snatched up the binoculars from her Operations Kit and stared out through the window across the bay towards Gull Island, her vision blurred by tears of frustration. Maybe Jack was right and they shouldn't waste any more time looking for the map – deep down, she couldn't believe that Mrs Loveday or Dotty had taken it anyway. Maybe they *should* just head out to Gull Island, before the map-thief beat them to it.

As she scanned the bay, Emily spotted a sailing boat. That wasn't so surprising – in good weather there were always sailing boats out on the bay. What *was* surprising was that this boat was heading directly towards the shallow waters around Gull Island, where the treacherous reefs were avoided by even the most experienced of sailors. Emily adjusted the focus on the binoculars and looked again at the boat. What she saw made her heart jump into her throat. The flag fluttering from the mast bore a familiar design of purple and yellow circles: the logo of Carrickstowe Marina. And there was a big green shape painted on the hull. She handed the binoculars to Jack. 'Do you see what I see?'

Jack peered through the binoculars. 'Er, it's a boat?'

'Not just any boat. It's from Carrickstowe Marina!'

Jack shrugged. 'So?' He turned back from the window and trained the binoculars on Scott's nose. 'Euggh! I can see right up your nostrils into your brain.'

Emily sighed. 'Simon Fox was hiring a boat from Carrickstowe Marina today.'

Jack made a puzzled face. 'OK, but how do you know that's him? Carrickstowe Marina probably hires out loads of boats.'

'I heard him make the booking over the phone this morning. He repeated the name of the boat they were giving him. It was called *Green Dolphin*!'

Scott grabbed the binoculars from Jack and looked out at the boat. 'You're right! That big green dolphin on the side *is* a bit of a giveaway.'

Jack shrugged. 'So what's the big deal? Simon Fox has gone out sailing for the day.'

'To *Gull Island*?' Emily snapped. Sometimes she was sure Jack acted dense just to wind her up. 'The hazardous rocks are marked on all the maps! Unless he's a *total* idiot and has got lost, he's got to have a very good reason for going there!'

Scott turned to Emily. 'You mean . . .'

'Yes,' Emily said. 'I *do* mean. He's searching for our gold!'

'No way!' Jack said. 'He wasn't even *there* when we found the treasure map. We've been through this before. He tried to go sailing and ended up mooching around Carrickstowe all day because of the storm.'

Scott frowned. 'He can't have been in Carrickstowe *all* day though. Remember Mrs Loveday said he bought her a Bakewell tart in Dotty's when they were sheltering from the storm?'

Jack laughed. 'OK, I admit that's a bit weird. Why would anyone want to "shelter" with Mrs Loveday? Let alone *encourage* her with cakes! But it's not a *crime*.'

Emily closed her eyes to shut out the boys' voices and cast her mind back to the day of the storm. When exactly had Simon appeared back at The Lighthouse? *We were looking at the map in the dining room, then Dad came in to set up for dinner and we cleared everything away. Simon appeared at the front door moments later. What if . . .*

'Hurry up!' she shouted, jumping off her bed and flying down the spiral stairs. 'Dining room . . . experiment . . .'

Experiment? Jack's imagination conjured up a picture of Emily in a white coat, her hair sticking out like a mad scientist's, telling him he wouldn't feel a thing as she inserted electrodes into his brain.

'Right,' Emily said, once they were all gathered in the dining room. 'You two sit at this table and pretend to be looking at the map. Just talk about it in normal voices . . . well, as *normal* as you can manage,' she added, looking at Jack.

Jack stared at her. 'And we're doing this because . . .'

'It's a *reconstruction*!' Emily explained. 'The dining

room window is right next to the front door. Maybe Simon Fox arrived back earlier than we thought. *Maybe* he overheard us talking about the gold as he was about to come in. Then he hung around, listening in from outside the window!'

Scott frowned. 'I see what you mean, but there were gale force winds. He couldn't have heard us. Not to mention the fact that he'd have been blown out to sea!'

'But the storm was over by the time he got back,' Jack pointed out.

'Exactly!' Emily hurried across the guest lounge and out of the front door. She looked in through the big conservatory windows and gave the boys a thumbs-up sign. They started talking and pointing at the imaginary map on the table. She *knew* they were talking because she could see their lips moving, but she couldn't hear a thing above the usual Castle Key soundtrack of ocean waves and seagulls; the thick reinforced glass in the windows blocked every sound. She went back inside. 'Can't hear you! Maybe you were talking too quietly?'

Jack shook his head. ' Any louder and we'd have been shouting. Let me try!'

So Jack went and stood outside the window while Scott and Emily talked at the table. He came back in shaking his head. 'The only way Simon Fox could have heard us from outside was if he's a trained lip-reader. '

But suddenly Scott leapt up so fast he knocked his chair over. 'I've got it!'

'Eughh! Is it infectious?' Jack asked, shrinking away from Scott.

Scott ignored him. 'Don't you remember, Em? Your mum came in and opened all the windows to let in some fresh air when the storm died down!'

'Of course! That's it!' Emily ran to the windows and helped Scott throw them all open. Then she dashed back outside. Drift scampered after her. He hadn't figured out the rules of this new running-in-and-out game yet, but it was fun!

'Gold, treasure, map, island . . . Can you hear us now?' Scott asked in a low voice.

'Every single word!'

The three friends looked at each other through the open window. There was a long moment of silence. A moment in which the terrible truth sank in. A moment in which they *knew* that Simon Fox had stolen the map as surely as if he'd left them a box of Quality Street and a thank-you note.

Jack sank his head into his hands. 'He seemed like such a great guy! He brought us chocolates! He talks to old ladies! Even the Hartley Horrors like him!'

Scott sighed. 'And he's been following us, hasn't he? It wasn't a coincidence that he turned up at Dotty's when we were talking to Old Bob about the shipwreck. And he was at the Ship and Anchor when we were asking Colin about the coins.'

Emily pressed her forehead against the warm stone

of the lighthouse wall as despair washed over her like seasickness. Even Drift licking the back of her knees wasn't helping. This entire investigation had been a disaster from start to finish. How could she have made so many basic mistakes? Overlooking an obvious suspect, leaving vital evidence lying around, slapdash security procedures ... All the time they'd been running around tailing perfectly innocent people, Simon Fox had been stalking *them*. Now, not only did he have their map, but he knew how to read the code and he knew which coin to use.

And he was on his way to Gull Island to find the gold!

Fourteen

The Race to Gull Island

Emily untied the mooring line and they all pushed *Gemini* out into the water, running alongside and hopping in like the start of an Olympic bobsleigh final. Drift jumped in last, his tail wagging like a metronome. There'd been a frenzy of activity as the friends had rushed around gathering equipment for the race to Gull Island: navigation charts, binoculars, bottles of water, emergency biscuit supplies raided from The Lighthouse kitchen, and the photo of the Kruger Pond, of course. Drift had no idea where they were going or why, but with a sea breeze blowing back his ears and spray in his nostrils, who cared?

Scott took the oars and rowed as if he was on the home straight in the Oxford–Cambridge Boat Race – although if he had been, of course, he'd have had seven other world-class rowers heaving away alongside him, which would have made the job much easier. It would also have been easier if their opponent hadn't had a huge head start! At least there'd been lots of chances for Scott to practise rowing since his feeble attempts on the way to the Whistling Caves when they first came to Castle Key. By now he was a skilled and powerful oarsman. He kept up a good speed, heading due west across the bay, but after fifteen minutes his muscles were on fire. He handed the oars to Jack and swigged from a bottle of water.

'How long will it take to get there?' he asked Emily.

'If we keep up this pace and the sea stays calm, it'll be another half an hour or so.' Emily lifted the binoculars to her eyes. 'It looks like Fox has anchored his sailing boat some way out from Gull Island. He must have a tender – a little dinghy or something – and be going ashore in that. *Grrr!* I was hoping he'd be dumb enough to sail too close and run aground on the rocks.'

'Hasn't he watched any films?' Jack panted between strokes. 'Doesn't he *know* baddies are meant to make stupid schoolboy errors?'

After half an hour of hard rowing, they drew level with the sailing boat. The *Green Dolphin* was swaying gently at anchor. As Emily had expected, the sails were furled and the tender was missing. She looked up at the craggy contours of Gull Island, its sheer cliffs streaked with white – like a giant cake drizzled with icing. She checked her map of the bay, onto which she'd pencilled Old Bob's notes about the best approach to the island. Then she grasped the oars and began to weave her way through the outlying rocks.

Suddenly Drift started barking.

'There he is!' Jack shouted over the barking and the screeching of thousands of gulls. A small inflatable dinghy was bobbing about in the rocks off the southernmost tip of the island.

Emily shaded her eyes from the glare of brilliant sunlight bouncing off the water and the white rocks. The man on board was definitely Simon Fox. Emily could make out his blond hair and faded blue shirt. He was caught up in a kind of mini-whirlpool inside a ring of rocks, as if he was in the spin cycle of a washing machine. His little boat had an outboard motor, but it must have broken down because he was wielding a paddle and, from the way he was behaving – not so much rowing as swatting at the water – he was clearly no oarsman. He was in trouble and starting to panic. But that wasn't the only thing that was bothering Emily.

'Oh, no! He's got the gold!' she cried.

'How do you know?' Scott shouted.

Emily pointed. 'Look how low the dinghy is in the water. It must be carrying a very heavy cargo.'

'What are we going to do?' Scott yelled.

But before Emily could answer, she heard a shout. Simon Fox was standing up in his boat – making it more unstable than ever – waving his arms and calling out, 'Help! Over here!'

'He must be kidding!' Jack snorted. 'Why would we help that gold-robbing weasel?'

'Well, we can't just leave him to drown,' Emily pointed out.

Scott took the oars and starting rowing towards Fox. 'No, but we'll make him agree to give us our gold back before we get him out of there.'

'Careful!' Emily cried. 'Don't get too close or we'll get sucked into that cauldron too.'

When they'd manoeuvred *Gemini* as close to the rocks as they dared, Emily uncoiled the mooring line and threw it to Simon Fox.

Hanging on to the side of his lurching dinghy, Fox tried to grab the rope with one hand. He missed and it splashed into the water. Emily gathered it in and tried again. On the fifth attempt Fox caught the end and tied it to the bow of his boat. Scott, Jack and Emily hauled the little dinghy out of the churning maelstrom. Once in calmer waters the friends helped Fox to wedge the boat into a crevice in the rocks next to *Gemini*.

Simon Fox puffed out his cheeks and rubbed his hands through his spiky blond hair – which was liberally splattered with white blobs. His face and neck were brick red with sunburn. 'Cheers, kids,' he shouted, flashing them a friendly grin. 'I thought I'd just mosey over and explore this island. Didn't realize the rocks were such a deathtrap!' He slapped his forehead. 'What a drongo, eh? Right landlubber I am! Lucky you guys came to my rescue.' He held up his hand for a high-five.

No one responded. Fox's smile faltered.

'Don't give us that rubbish!' Scott said. 'We know what you're up to. You nicked our treasure map and you've dug up our gold! Hand it over!'

Fox raised his sun-bleached eyebrows and laughed. 'Treasure map? Gold? Is this a game of *Pirates of the Caribbean?*'

'We *know* you've got it!' Jack told him.

Suddenly Simon Fox's jovial smile faded and he nodded sadly, as if disappointed with himself. He held his hands up in surrender. 'OK. It's a fair cop,' he sighed. 'I'll come quietly!'

'So you *did* steal our map!' Scott shouted.

'No, I just *borrowed* it. Look, I'm really sorry, kids, I should have told you. It's just that when I heard you talking about the gold, I didn't think you'd ever have a chance of actually being able to crack that code and find it yourself. I'm a bit of a metal detector buff, so I thought I'd see if I could track it down for you. *Obviously*, I was going to hand it over when I found it. I just thought it would make a great surprise for you all!'

Emily wasn't sure she believed him.

Fox looked her in the eye. Then he tapped his chest with both hands as if to show her that his heart was in the right place. 'OK! It was a dozy idea. My bad! I just haven't been thinking straight since my girlfriend left me . . . and now my dumb scheme has backfired and you all think I'm a right scumbag! Nice work, Fox!'

Scott and Jack laughed, and even Emily couldn't help being won round by Simon telling himself off. She was also starting to feel a little sorry for him. They'd ruined the surprise he'd planned. And at least he'd found the gold! She leaned across and peered over the side of the dinghy. But there was nothing there! No wooden chest with big brass hinges. Not even a scruffy old box. Just a metal detector lying in the ankle-deep water and a gash along the flank of the boat. An entire section of the wall had almost completely deflated. *That* was why the boat was sitting so low in the water. It was sinking! Emily stared at Fox. 'You *haven't* found the gold?'

Simon Fox shook his head. He pulled the treasure map out of his pocket and shook it. 'This map is a hoax. It's all wrong!'

'Wrong?' Scott asked. 'What do you mean?'

'It's not even the *shape* of this wretched island. I should know; I've been crawling around on the rocks for hours, getting cooked in the sun and ripping my knees to shreds while these damn birds use me for target practice. There's meant to be a little crescent-shaped bay on the south coast: it's not there! Nothing lines up with the map. It's a load of codswallop!'

Emily stared at him. This couldn't be right. After all their work, they'd been beaten to the gold and *then* it turned out the gold wasn't even there! She sank her head on her knees and pulled Drift close to hide the tears that were pricking her eyes.

'And this dinghy's a goner now,' Simon Fox went on. 'So can I bum a lift with you fellas back to the *Green Dolphin*?'

'Sure,' Scott said in a flat voice.

Fox climbed aboard *Gemini* and sat down. 'I think your William Maddox guy was having a laugh!' He held out the map as if about to toss it into the waves. In the sunlight the thick parchment was as transparent as tracing paper; the faded ink was much clearer than it had been in the light of the oil lamp on a dark, stormy afternoon.

Suddenly Emily saw something that made her heart miss a beat. One tiny dot she hadn't noticed before. One tiny dot that made a huge difference! She lunged for the map, snatched it from Fox's hand and held it up to the light again. 'Look!' She waved the map at Scott and Jack. 'There's a full stop after *Gull*. It's an abbreviation! It's not *Gull* Island at all. The gold's hidden on *Gulliver's* Island!'

Fifteen

A Pirates' Charter

Emily wished she could snatch the words out of the air and stuff them back in her mouth as soon as she'd said them. She glanced at Scott and Jack. She could tell they were thinking the same thing. If she'd kept it zipped, they could have dumped Fox back at his boat, then gone to Gulliver's Island on their own. But now *he* knew the real location too! It wouldn't be half as much fun finding the treasure with a spare adult tagging along.

'*Gulliver's* Island, you say?' Fox asked. 'Where's that?'

'Oh, it's miles away. We can't get there today,' Emily said, trying to put him off the scent.

But Fox took a small map of the bay from his shirt pocket. 'No, it's not far, look!' The boys looked. Emily didn't bother. She knew perfectly well where Gulliver's Island was. Half a mile or so to the south, it was twice the size of Gull Island and home to an old abandoned monastery. It was also much closer to where Old Bob said *The Empress* had gone down all those years ago. Now she thought about it, it made much more sense that it was the island where Maddox's lifeboat had washed up.

'Hey, I've got a great idea, kids,' Fox said. 'Why don't we join forces and find that gold? If we set off now there'll be time before dark. *I've* got the metal detector. *You've* got the boat. Together we make one hell of a team!'

Jack eyed Simon Fox warily. He seemed genuine enough and he *had* brought them chocolates and shared his bacon sandwich. But wasn't this the same guy who had 'borrowed' their map without asking?

Fox grinned and clapped Jack on the back. 'Don't worry, mate! I'm not expecting a share of the gold. It's just the challenge I'm up for, the thrill of the chase! And after we've found it, we can all go back to the *Green Dolphin* for a celebratory picnic and sail home in triumph. What do you say?'

Sounds fair enough, Jack thought. If Fox wasn't asking for a share of the gold, what did they have to lose? And they could use some help with the rowing. His arms still felt like marshmallow after their sprint across the bay. 'OK, I'm in!' he said.

Fox punched his arm. 'Good on ya!'

'How do we know we can trust you?' Scott asked.

Fox grinned. 'Read my lips! *I do not want your gold.* I'll put it in writing if you like.'

Scott looked at Emily. He had to admit, he was dying to get to Gulliver's Island. And it would be useful to have the metal detector with them. He nodded. Emily nodded back.

Emily rummaged in the waterproof bag of supplies and found a pen. Then she wrote on the back of the print-out of the Kruger Pond: *I, Simon Fox, solemnly swear that I will make no claim to any gold hidden by William Maddox on Gulliver's Island.* She handed the paper and pen to Fox. 'Sign this and date it, please.'

'I *was* joking!' Fox laughed. 'But OK, if you insist!' He took the pen and scrawled his signature, then looked up and grinned. 'It's like a Pirates' Charter.'

Jack liked that idea. 'Yeah! We should all sign it in blood.'

Fox laughed. 'Let's shake on it instead!' He spat into his palm and held out his hand. They all shook.

'What are we waiting for?' Fox asked. 'Let's go bag us some gold!' He hoisted the metal detector out of the

119

dinghy and stowed it in the bottom of *Gemini*. 'I'll take first shift on the oars.'

—

As they approached Gulliver's Island, the towers and arches of the ruined monastery were silhouetted against the late afternoon sun. Jack could hardly contain his excitement as they rowed into shore and moored *Gemini* to a chimney of rock.

Emily checked Maddox's map. 'This definitely looks like the place the lifeboat landed. Look where he's marked with his arrow – it's the end of this little cove. And these squiggles we thought were rocks or cliffs are the ruins.'

The three friends gathered on the stony beach and pored over the treasure map, while Drift – ecstatic to be back on dry land after the long sea voyage – raced around on the rocks. Simon Fox seemed happy to let the kids work out the map clues while he sat on a rock trying to dry off the metal detector with his shirt.

'Let's find the starting point,' Emily suggested. '*Point nose to nearest of the two towers and with both in alignment . . .*' she read aloud from the map.

'OK, so we should be able to see across the bay to Castle Key and line up the lighthouse and the castle,' Scott said, scrambling up onto the rocks.

Jack followed him. But there was just one minor problem: the monastery ruins were slap bang in the way.

To see the lighthouse or the castle from here, Maddox must either have been twenty feet tall or have had X-ray vision.

'I don't believe it,' Emily sighed. 'Surely we haven't got the wrong island *again*!'

So far, Jack was not impressed with Gulliver's Island. OK, the gulls weren't as deafening here. But who gave those monks planning permission to block his view with a stinking great monastery? And could someone stop that bell clanging in the wind? It was as if they'd been followed by the Castle Key bell-ringers!

Jack looked up and saw that the ringing was coming from an old bell tower on the edge of the monastery. Bell *tower*! Suddenly it hit him. He looked back at the ruins. Yes, there was a second rickety old tower behind them. He grabbed the photo of the Kruger Pond out of Scott's hand and scrambled across the rocks, pointing Kruger's nose at the bell tower. He zig-zagged side to side like a drunken hermit crab until he found the point where the two towers were lined up perfectly one behind the other. Then he waved his hands in the air and yelled, 'The nose has landed!' When the others ran to join him, he pointed at the monastery and took a bow. 'Ladies and gentlemen, I give you two towers in alignment.'

Emily threw her arms round him. 'Jack, you're a genius!'

Scott grinned. 'Yeah, he just does a good job of hiding it most of the time!'

Simon Fox clambered over the rocks with his metal detector. 'Nice work, mate!'

Jack soaked up the praise. It was long overdue. Scott had been getting far too much of the limelight lately, what with the whole Teenage Hero gig and then cracking the coin code – and Emily was *always* coming up with brilliant plans and ideas. 'Right,' he said, 'I'm on a roll. Next clue, please!'

Sixteen

Teamwork

Emily consulted the map. 'The next note says ... *and with S at shark* ... This must give us the second bearing so we can get in the right spot to start pacing out the directions.'

'That must be the S in the word AFRIKAANSCHE on the coin,' Scott said, 'which means it's over in that direction.' He pointed off towards the open sea.

Jack looked across the water as if expecting a triangular

fin to cruise past. He hummed a few bars of the theme from *Jaws*. 'Obviously it can't be a *real* shark,' he said. 'You don't get sharks in Cornwall!'

'Yes you do,' Emily said.

'Yeah, Great Whites,' Scott added. 'Enormous savage *hungry* ones!'

'No way!' Jack stared at his brother. 'You mean we've been rowing around shark-infested waters in that tiny little boat!'

Emily laughed. 'Don't listen to Scott. They're *basking* sharks. They only eat plankton!'

Simon grinned. 'If you want the really big man-eaters, come to Australia!'

'Anyway,' Emily said, turning her attention back to the map, 'Maddox can't mean a *real* shark swimming around in the sea. It wouldn't exactly be a helpful reference point.'

'More likely something in the *shape* of a shark,' Scott said.

Like what? Jack thought. Apart from the monastery, there was nothing here but a load of old . . . 'Rocks?' he mumbled.

'What about that one?' Emily pointed to a huge rock jutting up from the water just off the coast. 'If we walk closer to the monastery it'll be at the right angle.'

They headed inland up a steep slope away from the shoreline. Straggly weeds with pink flowers were sprouting up among the scattered boulders of the monastery ruins. The freshening breeze rustled the long dry grass and the bell tolled louder.

Any minute now, Jack thought, *we'll hear the ghostly chanting of a procession of hooded monks. I don't envy Maddox being here on a dark and stormy night!*

'It doesn't look much like a shark to me . . .' Scott said.

Emily marched on. They were almost in the shadow of the monastery now. She looked back at the rock. Scott was right. But, with your eyes half closed and a lot of imagination it *could* be a shark leaping out of the water. Then again, it could also be a banana or a bird . . . or just a curved rock. She took a step and looked again. *Then she saw it!* The pointed summit of a second rock in the distance poked up behind the 'shark' and made a perfect fin!

'This is it!' she shouted, grabbing the photo of the coin from Scott. 'We've got both bearings!' She lined up Kruger's nose with the two towers and the S with the shark rock. 'This is the starting point!'

Scott and Jack hugged her and they jumped up and down. Drift ran around in circles. He could feel the buzz of anticipation in the air.

Simon Fox high-fived them all. 'Great teamwork, guys!'

Emily was so excited she could hardly hold the coin print-out steady as Jack took the map and called out the first instruction. 'F6!' Together they all marched six paces in the direction of the F.

'Z4!' Jack shouted. They all turned towards the Z and took four steps.

Only a few moments later they had paced out the seventh and final step. They were standing in a bramble patch next to a heap of boulders. 'It must be here somewhere,' Emily breathed.

'Let's give the technology a whirl.' Simon switched on the metal detector and began to sweep it from side to side. There was a crackle and a fizz and then a loud bang. Fox swore and leaped back, clutching his hand. 'Damn! Electric shock! The seawater's short-circuited the sensors!'

'Never mind,' Emily said. 'Look at Drift!' The little dog was snuffling at the base of a massive boulder, scratching at the thin soil with his paws.

'Drift hasn't got water in *his* sensors!' Jack laughed. 'Come on, it must be under there.'

Together they leaned their weight against the boulder. They pushed and pushed. Scott was glad they had Simon with them now. They'd never have shifted the boulder without him.

'Timberrrrr!' Jack shouted as the rock finally toppled over.

They all fell to their knees and joined Drift scraping away at the thin dry soil. Suddenly Scott's hand hit something hard. *This was it!* A little more frantic scraping and the top of a wooden chest came into view. They reached down and cleared more earth away until they could drag it out of the hole. It was very heavy. For a moment everyone stared at the blackened wood and rusty hinges.

'Well, are we just going to look at it all day or are we going to open it?' Jack demanded.

'What if it's locked?' Scott asked.

'Maddox didn't *say* anything about a key . . .' Emily said.

'Only one way to find out!' Jack grabbed the lid. To his amazement, it creaked open.

The chest was full to the brim of big fat gold coins glinting in the late afternoon sunlight.

'Kruger Ponds!' Scott shouted. 'Thousands of them!'

Emily cuddled Drift. 'Drift did it again. He's always right!'

'Awesome!' Jack breathed.

Simon whistled. 'These little beauties must be worth a fortune!'

Suddenly they were all laughing and hugging each other – even Simon Fox. All the friends' earlier doubts about him were long since forgotten in the thrill of the discovery. *They had found the buried treasure!*

They all scooped up handfuls of gold coins and let them run through their fingers like golden waterfalls. Drift stood with his front paws on the edge of the chest and barked triumphantly.

After admiring the gold for some time, Scott happened to glance back into the hole. There was something else hidden in the space beneath the boulder. He bent down and unearthed a smaller, metal box, laid it down next to the chest and pulled open the lid. Inside was a rifle. Its slim wooden stock was badly scratched and dark with age, but its long barrel still looked mean.

'Wow! *Cool,* an old gun!' Jack said.

'Maddox must have brought his trusty weapon back from the Boer War,' Fox remarked. 'Nice-looking piece. A Lee-Enfield, by the look of it . . .' He picked up the gun and turned it over in his hands. 'They had a detachable magazine . . . This was state of the art in those days . . . Ah, yes, here it is.' Fox took the magazine out of the box and examined it briefly. 'Mmm, only four rounds left in here.' He fixed it to the top of the rifle.

Emily wasn't even remotely interested in guns. She looked at her watch and then at the orange disc of the sun sinking steadily towards the horizon. 'We need to get moving. It'll be dark soon.'

Scott reached for the handle at one end of the chest. 'It's going to be a killer lugging this over the rocks to *Gemini.* Give us a hand, Simon . . .'

Fox reached down. But he didn't take hold of the handle. Instead he held up the rifle and cocked it. He took a step back, curled his finger round the trigger and pointed the barrel at Scott.

Jack laughed. *He must think we're still playing at pirates . . .*

But then he saw the look on Fox's face and his laughter withered away.

Simon Fox was *deadly* serious. He'd double-crossed them again!

Seventeen

Welcome to the Real World

Fox narrowed his eyes and looked down the barrel of the gun. 'You kids think you're pretty smart, don't you?' His voice was hard and cold as the blade of a knife. 'You did a good job of figuring out those clues, I'll give you that. But now we're going to start playing by *my* rules!'

Jack stared at Fox. The friendly smile had transformed

into a sneer. It was as if he'd peeled off a mask to reveal a totally different person underneath.

'You kids are going to help me stow this gold on your rowing boat. But that's where it ends. I take the boat. You stay on the island.'

Emily opened her mouth to speak but Fox jerked the gun in her direction. 'As long as you all do *exactly* what I say, no one will get hurt. Don't worry! As soon as I'm out of here I'll call the coastguard. They'll come and pick you up.'

'But you agreed not to take any of the gold,' Emily said bravely, even though her voice was quavering.

Fox barked out a bitter laugh. 'Oh, yeah, honour among pirates, eh? What are you going to do – make me walk the plank?'

'You signed a contract.' Scott kept his eyes fixed on the gun – as if it was a rattlesnake about to strike. 'And you shook on it!'

Fox laughed again. 'Yeah, well, here's a surprise for you, kids! I lied. Welcome to the real world. *People tell lies!* I need a lot of dosh in a hurry. And now I've got it.' He looked down at the chest of gold. 'Now, let's shift this lot onto the boat. You boys should be able to carry it between you.'

Jack's fury flamed as hot and bright as a blowtorch. How *dare* Fox double-cross them again like this? They'd rescued him from drowning *and* given him a second chance after he'd nicked their map. Didn't he know the meaning of *gratitude*? *If this guy thinks we're going to help him walk away with our treasure, he can think again.*

'Move it!' Fox snapped, pointing at the chest with the gun.

On the other hand, he does have a Lee-Enfield rifle pointed right at us, Jack thought. *That does kind of change things.* He stared at the gun. It looked like something in a display cabinet at the War Museum. *Hang on,* Jack thought, *it is a museum piece! It's been underground for over a hundred years. Surely the gunpowder in those cartridges will have got damp in all that time. And the metal's all rusty. There's no way that gun's going to fire! Look what happened to the metal detector after one quick dunking in the sea.*

Jack glanced at Scott and Emily. They were standing either side of him, still staring at Psycho-Fox, both motionless as living statues without the silver paint. Drift was sitting at Emily's feet, a soft growl bubbling in his throat

Fox took a step forward.

No way! Jack thought. He grabbed hold of Emily and Scott by the elbows and began to run, dragging them with him. 'Come on!' he yelled, 'Fox is just bluffing. That gun won't fire!'

Scott's heart almost burst out of his ribcage. What was Jack doing? Fox had a gun pointed at them! Did Jack really think he could outrun a speeding bullet?

Only Jack could be crazy enough . . . but there was no time to think. Now Emily was running as well, holding on to Jack. Drift was sprinting along next to them. Scott had no choice. If he pulled Jack back now they would just be in more danger.

'OK, make for the monastery,' he gasped, pushing Jack and Emily ahead of him, trying to shield them with his body from the gunfire he was sure would come at any second. He saw a low tumbledown wall at the base of the monastery ruins. It was only a few metres ahead. *If we can just get behind it and take cover* . . .

'Hurry, Drift!' Emily yelled. She knew they were running for their lives. She was furious with herself for having let Simon Fox take her in with that buddy-buddy act *again*. How could she have been so gullible? She should have listened to Drift. He'd never been that keen on him. She looked back over her shoulder to see Fox raise the gun to his shoulder and take aim. Still she ran. The dry grass tore at her legs and her bare feet stumbled over the scattered rocks and hidden potholes.

Time seemed to slow as she felt Scott pull her arm. She dived headfirst behind the wall as she heard the click of the trigger behind her.

A blast of pain slammed through her body.

For a second she saw Scott and Jack's faces at the end of a pulsating tunnel of light. Then everything went dark.

Eighteen

Scott Hatches a Plan

'Oh my God! He's killed Emily!' Jack screamed. He stared down at his friend, lying motionless among the rubble and scrubby weeds. Her skin had the greenish white tinge of fish scales and her eyes were half-closed. Drift was whimpering, pawing at Emily's arm and licking her face.

Scott took hold of her shoulders and shook her gently. 'Emily, can you hear me?'

'What are you *doing*?' Jack yelled. He could feel tears running down his face.

'She's not dead!' Scott hissed. 'Fox didn't even fire the gun. Did you *hear* a shot?'

Jack hastily wiped the tears away with the back of his hand. He could see now the shallow rise and fall of Emily's collarbone above the neck of her white t-shirt. She was breathing. There was no bullet hole, no ooze of scarlet blood.

'She's fainted!' Scott said. 'Maybe it's from fear.'

Emily's eyelids flickered. 'I did *not* faint from fear!' she spat through gritted teeth. 'Drift, stop!' Emily laughed as he slobbered on her face. 'I twisted my ankle on a rock when I dived for the wall. I must have passed out with the pain.' She attempted a small wiggle of her foot to check how things were doing down there. 'Agggh!' Not good. It felt as if someone was shattering her ankle bone with a giant hammer. 'I'm OK,' she said, levering herself up with her arms, wincing at the twist of pain that accompanied every move. 'What's Fox doing now?'

Scott peeped over the wall. 'He's dragging the chest across the rocks.'

'If Psycho-Fox thinks he's making off with our gold ...' Jack started to climb over the wall. 'Come on! If we all charge down there we could overpower him with the element of surprise.'

Scott grabbed Jack's t-shirt and pulled him back

down. 'Are you off your head? You nearly got us all shot once already.'

'I *knew* that gun wouldn't work,' Jack retorted. 'The gunpowder's damp.'

Scott stared at Jack. 'It *could* have been kept perfectly dry in that metal box. We were just lucky! Next time it could go off!'

Fox must have heard the scuffle behind the wall. He looked up from hauling the chest. 'I'm not going to waste my time chasing you lot,' he shouted. 'I want to get out of here before dark. You can stay put until the coastguard gets here.'

Jack slid back down the wall and sat leaning against the rough stones. This was unbearable. There had to be *something* they could do. Suddenly he had an idea. If Psycho-Fox could call the coastguard, why couldn't *they*? In fact, while they were at it, they could call Detective Inspector Hassan at Carrickstowe police station and tip off the police to arrest Fox when he tried to return the *Green Dolphin* to the marina. All they needed was a mobile phone. He didn't have one himself, but Scott and Emily never went anywhere without theirs . . . 'Phone!' he blurted.

'Of course!' Emily's face lit up, but then it dimmed again. 'Oh, no, I left it in the waterproof bag on *Gemini*!'

Scott grinned. 'But I didn't!' He whipped his phone out of his pocket and started jabbing at the keypad. Then he sank his head in his hands and tugged at his

137

hair. 'I don't believe it! No reception!' This was the last straw! Scott was so frustrated he couldn't even look at the other two. 'Come on,' he muttered to Jack. 'Let's get Emily inside the monastery. It's getting dark.' Together, they half-walked, half-carried her through the arched doorway and made her comfortable on a moss-covered bench.

The gloom of the deserted monastery reflected Scott's mood. Long shadows from the setting sun were collecting in the corners. Hands thrust in pockets, he left Emily with Drift and Jack and wandered miserably across a courtyard bordered by crumbling pillars. He entered a cavernous hall. Narrow tables and benches were blanketed in dust. There was even an old metal goblet and plate lying in the corner.

He mooched along a covered walkway to a row of cell-like rooms, each with a small wooden bed and a cross nailed to the wall above it. He sank down on a bed. The room was swathed in cobwebs and the small furry bodies of bats hung from the stone ceiling. Scott shuddered. This place was *creepy* – as if the ancient monks would be returning any moment to find him trespassing. He was about to hurry away when the door slammed shut in the breeze. For a terrifying moment he thought he was trapped in the dark cell. But the door creaked open when he pushed against it. There was a big old metal key in the lock. Without really thinking, he reached out and turned it back and forth. The lock still worked.

That's when the idea came to him.

No, it's too complicated, he told himself. *Fox will never fall for it.* But what did they have to lose? Well, their lives, if Fox managed to get that gun working again, but apart from that . . . And it could just work!

Scott hurried back to Jack, Emily and Drift and knelt down next to them. 'I've thought of a way we might be able to trap Fox on the island while we get away with the gold,' he whispered. 'We just need to trick him into entering the monastery.'

Emily smiled but then she shook her head. 'You heard him. He's not going to bother chasing us.'

'He might if he thinks we're phoning the police,' Scott said.

'Hello! Have you lost your memory or something?' Jack said. 'No reception!'

Scott rolled his eyes. '*I* know that, *you* know that, but *Fox* doesn't know that, does he?'

Emily was starting to look intrigued. 'So what are you thinking?'

'OK, this is what we do. But we've got to be fast.' Hastily Scott outlined his plan.

When he'd finished, Jack stared at him in disbelief. 'That,' he said, 'is the most totally and utterly *insane* plan I've ever heard!' Then he grinned. 'Count me in!'

'Me too,' Emily said. 'But I might need a bit of a hand.'

Scott and Jack pulled Emily up and helped her hobble

to the cell with the key in the door. They sat down on the old bed. 'Somehow, we've got to lure him in here,' Scott said.

'One of us could be pretending to talk to the police on the mobile,' Jack suggested. 'He comes running in. We slam the door behind him. Job done!'

'Any volunteers to be the one who gets trapped in here with him? No, I thought not,' Scott snapped. He could see his plan unravelling in front of his eyes like a sleeve with a pulled thread.

But Emily jumped in and started to knit it back together. 'No, wait! I've got an idea. Scott, you've got a voice recorder on your phone, haven't you? We'll record a *fake* conversation with the police, then put it on PLAY and leave it in here. We might lose the phone but at least we'll all be on the outside!'

They were back on track! 'Brilliant!' Scott said. 'OK, Em, you record the message, then leave the phone in here and hide in the next room. Can you make it that far on your own?'

'Of course I can,' Emily said. 'I'll hop if I have to!'

'While you do that, Jack and I will go back behind that wall and have a loud argument about calling the police. If we're lucky Fox is still close enough to hear us. That should get him up here like a shot!'

'Yeah,' Emily said with a grimace. 'It's the *shot* part I'm worried about!'

'Come on, let's do it!' Jack shouted.

The boys sprinted out of the monastery. There was no time to lose.

—

Scott peeked over the low wall. Simon Fox had hauled the chest halfway to the shore, but was now sitting on it, having a rest. It was hard to tell whether he was still within earshot, but they had to give it a try. 'WHAT DO YOU MEAN YOU DROPPED THE PHONE?' Scott yelled at the top of his voice.

'I HAD IT A MINUTE AGO!' Jack bellowed back.

'IF WE DON'T FIND THAT PHONE WE CAN'T CALL THE POLICE!'

Jack glanced over the wall. Psycho-Fox was looking up towards the wall, frowning. 'Keep going,' he hissed to Scott. 'I think he's heard us.'

'IT MUST BE HERE SOMEWHERE!' Scott shouted.

'IT IS!' Jack cried. 'I'VE FOUND IT!'

'DIAL NINE, NINE, NINE! QUICKLY!'

Jack looked over the wall again. *Simon Fox had taken the bait!* He was running up the slope towards them. In the twilight, Jack could make out the shape of the rifle in his hand.

'Oh, no, you don't!' Fox yelled. 'Give me that phone!'

'Run for it!' Jack grabbed Scott's arm and they bolted into the monastery.

Meanwhile, Emily had been at work in the cell. First she sat for a moment and closed her eyes. The throbbing in her ankle was getting worse. She'd been determined not to let the boys know how bad it was, but she felt dizzy, as if she might be sick any minute. *I have to focus . . .*

Drift whimpered sympathetically. Emily took a deep breath and pressed RECORD on Scott's phone. 'Hello,' she said in a loud voice, 'Carrickstowe police station? I'd like to report a robbery . . . a man called Simon Fox . . . yes, the police please. I'm on Gulliver's Island . . . That's right, Simon Fox . . . We need the coastguard . . .' She kept talking into the phone as long as she dared. Then she eased herself down from the bed, placing all her weight on her good leg. Timing was everything. She had to leave herself long enough to get out of the room, but if she pressed PLAY on the phone too soon, the message might finish before Fox got close enough to hear it. Clinging to the wall for balance, she made her way to the door. Then she turned the volume to maximum, pressed PLAY and slid the phone across the floor into the back corner of the room. 'Come on, Drift,' she said. 'Let's get out of here!'

Nineteen

Got You Now!

With the last of her strength, Emily hopped inside the first door she came to and leaned against the wall, cold beads of sweat running down between her shoulder blades. Seconds later, Scott and Jack piled in behind her.

'Is he coming?' Emily gasped.

'Yeah, right behind us,' Jack told her.

They all listened. Fox's footsteps could be heard

echoing around the cloisters. 'Where've you gone, you little cane toads?' he yelled.

The footsteps grew fainter.

'He's gone the wrong way!' Scott groaned. 'We've got to get him back before the phone message runs out.'

As if he understood Scott's words, Drift darted out from behind Emily and ran towards the booby-trapped cell growling and barking.

'Aha! Got you now!' Fox yelled.

Scott put his finger to his lips.

Jack rolled his eyes. *Like I need to be* told *to keep quiet when there's a crazed, gun-toting Australian gold-thief hunting us down.* He pressed himself against the wall.

'*Carrickstowe police station?*' Emily's voice was still playing on the phone. '*I'd like to report a robbery . . .*'

'OH, NO, YOU DON'T!' Fox yelled, charging into the empty room to stop her.

'Now!' Jack shouted. He ran out into the walkway and rammed his shoulder against the door to Fox's room. Scott was right beside him. Jack caught a glimpse of Fox's face as he turned round, eyes darting side to side, searching for Emily. He could *hear* her, but there was nobody there! Next second, confusion was replaced by ice-cold fury as Fox realized he'd been tricked into the cell. He lunged for the boys.

Scott and Jack threw their weight against the door. But in the split second before it closed, Jack saw something in the cell that made him jump back in horror. Drift had chased Fox inside and was now snarling round his legs.

'STOP!' Jack shouted to Scott. 'Drift's in there!'

'DRIIIIIIFT!' Scott and Jack yelled in frantic chorus. 'Come *here*!'

Drift leapt through the door. Scott and Jack pushed again but now the door wouldn't close. Psycho-Fox had wedged his foot in the gap. Without stopping to think, Jack kicked the foot as hard as he could. The door slammed shut. Scott turned the key.

Jack looked at Scott. 'We did it!'

Scott grinned. 'We *actually* did it!' Then he shook his head. 'Come on, we've got to hurry up. If Fox gets that gun working he can shoot the lock off.' He broke off as Fox roared like a wounded lion and began to pound on the other side of the door. 'If he doesn't break the door down first!'

There was a crunch of splintering plastic as Scott's mobile phone was hurled against the wall.

'And we definitely don't want to be around when he gets out!'

Jack looked up to see Emily propped against the wall behind him. She held up her hand for a high-five. 'Good work!' she said.

She was smiling. But her hand was clammy and she was so pale that blue veins showed beneath her skin. Her brown eyes looked too big for her face, like a character in a *Manga* cartoon.

'Come on,' Scott said, 'you look like something out of the House of Horrors. I'll give you a piggy-back to *Gemini*!'

'My Teenage Hero!' Jack laughed.

As they hurried across the courtyard, Jack couldn't resist throwing Psycho-Fox's own words back at him. 'Don't worry,' he called over his shoulder, 'as soon as we're out of here we'll call the coastguard to come and pick you up!'

Fox was still hammering on the door. Jack couldn't blame him; he wouldn't fancy being locked in that cell with the spiders and the bats as darkness fell either!

＿

Scott ferried Emily to the boat and then ran back up the beach to help Jack with the chest of gold. Even with two of them it was like being in training for the World Weightlifting Championships. The light was dwindling fast now. Emily had found the emergency torch on *Gemini* and was holding it up to guide them to the boat.

'Watch out!' Jack complained. 'The corner's jabbing my leg. I'm going to be covered in bruises!'

'Just get a move on,' Scott snapped back. 'You'll have bullet holes to worry about if Fox gets that rifle working, let alone bruises.'

'Stop going on about that stupid gun,' Jack said. 'I told you. The gunpowder is dam—'

CRACK!

The words died on Jack's tongue as the shot rang out, bouncing round the walls of the monastery ruins.

'You were saying?' Scott panted.

Jack grimaced. 'OK. Let's just hurry. If he's managed to shoot the lock off, he'll be out of there any second!'

They were on the last stretch now. Arms burning, legs straining, backs breaking, the boys hauled the chest over the beach. At last they were wading into the water.

Another gunshot split the night. And then another.

With their last shreds of strength, Scott and Jack hoisted the chest over the side of the boat.

Emily pulled it in as best she could, the surge of adrenaline blotting out the pain. She began to push off from the shore while the boys and Drift scrambled on board.

Scott took the oars and rowed as hard as he could. But they were not far from the shore when Emily shone the torch back at the island to see Fox running down the beach towards them. He was brandishing the rifle.

'Duck!' Emily yelled, pulling Drift down from the bow.

Jack tucked his head onto his knees. 'How many rounds did Fox say were in that magazine?'

'Four,' Emily replied.

'How many has he fired?'

'Four,' Scott said. 'I think.'

'You *think*?' Jack asked.

'Scott's right,' Emily said. 'He fired one at us when we ran and three more just now.'

Jack straightened up and looked back. In the torch-light, Fox was aiming the gun straight at him.

Twenty

The Ghost Ship

*C*rack!

The bullet whizzed past Jack's ear.

Emily's hand flew to her mouth as Scott grabbed Jack and yanked him into the bottom of the boat.

'I was wrong,' Scott muttered. 'He'd only used three rounds. That first shot he took didn't work, remember? The bullet jammed in the magazine but didn't fire! Jack, are you OK?'

Jack put his hand to his ear. It was still there. Yes, he was OK. In fact, he felt strangely elated. That bullet had had his name on it, but it had missed its target, and, by all calculations, Fox was now out of ammo. Jack had cheated death and lived to tell the tale. He was tempted to wind Scott and Emily up by pretending his ear had been shot off and his brains were spilling out. But he knew they didn't have time for messing around. He sighed. What a waste of an opportunity! 'Yeah, I'm fine. Just double-check your figures next time! If I want my ears pierced I can think of better ways to do it!'

Emily laughed with relief. She shone the torch back at Fox. He had discarded the gun and was running down the beach. As she watched, he plunged into the waves. 'I don't believe it, he's swimming after us!'

Scott grabbed the oars and began to row again.

Emily glanced ahead. 'Look out!' she shouted, now directing the torch towards a row of snaggle-toothed rocks poking up out of the water. The waves were tossing the boat towards them. Scott pulled *Gemini* clear with just an oar's width to spare.

In the torch's narrow beam Emily picked out the lonely figure of Simon Fox thrashing through the waves towards them. He was clearly a strong swimmer.

'Faster!' Jack urged. 'He's gaining on us!'

'We can't,' Emily cried. 'It's like an obstacle course with these rocks!'

'And my arms are killing me!' Scott groaned.

Jack swapped places and took the oars.

Emily arced the torch back and forth like a searchlight, lighting the way ahead, then checking Fox's progress. He was so close now she could see his face when he looked up from the water. *He's going to catch us . . .* she thought. But then, all of a sudden, he was gone. *A rogue current must have dragged him down beneath the waves. Or a shark?* Emily's fevered imagination was starting to take over. 'He's vanished!' she shouted. 'We can't let him drown. We'll have to go back and help him. But what if he attacks us again?'

'No, there he is!' Scott cried, directing her hand with the torch. Fox's head had popped back up in the trough between two waves. Emily shivered. He seemed to stare right into her eyes before he turned and started swimming slowly back towards Gulliver's Island.

'He's given up!' Scott exclaimed in relief.

'Welcome to the real world, mate!' Jack shouted after the retreating figure.

━

They rowed on through the dark. The lights of Castle Key village twinkled on the other side of the bay, but they didn't seem to be getting any closer. Scott tried not to think about *The Empress* – and all the other ships that had foundered on the rocks in the bay and were now lying on the seabed, full of skeletons, many fathoms below. Emily had tried her mobile phone but there was still no reception. Scott could tell she was worried about her parents. They'd be frantic by now; it was dark and *Gemini* was missing. Aunt Kate had probably noticed the boys were late home too.

'Should we send up an emergency flare?' Jack asked.

'Yeah … no … maybe … I dunno!' Emily murmured.

Scott looked at Jack. Emily was many things but indecisive wasn't one of them. They'd *never* known her not have an opinion before! She must be in a seriously bad way. They'd made her drink some water and nibble at one of the biscuits they'd packed, but she was still weak and exhausted. Scott grabbed the waterproof bag and starting looking for a flare.

'Hang on, what's that?' Jack shouted. 'A massive great rock! Dead ahead!'

But it wasn't a rock. The silhouette of a sailing boat loomed out of the night, dark and deserted as a ghost ship. The torch beam illuminated a flag with purple and yellow circles flying from the mast.

'It's the *Green Dolphin*,' Scott cried. 'Fox's boat!'

'Oh, yes!' Jack shouted. 'I say we board this vessel and claim it for our own!'

Scott nodded. 'We can use the radio to call the coast-guard.'

Scott and Jack tied Gemini alongside the *Green Dolphin* and manhandled – and dog-handled – Emily and Drift up the stepladder and into the small cabin.

Jack made Emily as comfortable as possible with her foot propped up on the seat. He found a cool box and extracted a cold bottle of water which he placed gently under her ankle. Then he wrapped her in a blanket.

Meanwhile, Scott found the radio. He checked the instruction chart displayed on the wall and scrolled to channel sixteen, the emergency frequency.

'You have to shout *mayday, mayday, mayday*!' Jack said.

'No!' Emily cried. 'That's only if we're about to sink!'

Scott scanned the information and found what he was looking for. 'Coastguard, coastguard, coastguard . . .' he said into the transmitter. 'This is *Green Dolphin*, *Green Dolphin*, *Green Dolphin*. We're anchored off Gull Island . . .'

—

While they waited for the lifeboat to arrive, Scott switched on the white warning light at the top of the mast to prevent other boats running into them, and Jack located the food supplies.

'Remember that celebration picnic Fox promised us,' he said, arranging a banquet of cheese, salami, tortilla chips and cans of Coke on the tiny fold-out table. 'Well, here it is!'

'Cheers!' Emily laughed, raising her can of Coke. She was starting to revive now that the cold water-bottle was numbing her ankle and she knew they were safe. She broke off a piece of cheese and fed it to Drift. 'Of course, we'll be drinking out of expensive crystal glasses soon!'

'On our private plane . . .' Jack put in, clinking his can against Emily's in a toast.

'And flying to our palace on a tropical island,' Scott added, dipping his tortilla chip into a jar of spicy salsa.

Jack raised his Coke can again. 'Here's to Psycho-Fox. At least he hauled that chest halfway to the boat for us. I hope he's enjoying his stay on Gulliver's island.'

Scott nodded. 'Yeah, I was *so* tempted to "forget" to tell the coastguard about him and leave him locked in that cell all night!'

Emily grinned. 'I suppose we *will* have to hand the gold over to the police . . .'

'No way!' Jack had a much better idea. 'We sail off into the night instead, before the coastguard finds us. We've got the gold. We're millionaires! We can do *anything*!' He pictured himself wandering onto the verandah of his palace, glancing down at the row of shiny sports cars parked among the palm trees. Should he go for a swim in his Olympic-size infinity pool first, or test out his new bike on the custom-built indoor BMX track? Decisions, decisions . . .

'Let's splice the mainsail, raise the anchor, and run with the wind!' Jack had no idea what any of that meant, but it sounded good.

Scott and Emily were shaking their heads. 'We were only joking!' Emily said. 'We have to hand it over.'

'What?' Jack asked in a small voice. 'All of it?'

'Yes, *all* of it,' Emily told him. 'Otherwise we're no better than Simon Fox.'

'And,' Scott pointed out, 'if we stole the gold, we'd be on the run for the rest of our lives.'

Jack thought that sounded quite fun, but he could see he wasn't winning the argument. He sighed and took a gold coin out of his pocket and placed it on the table. 'I guess I'll just have to wait for my reward!'

Suddenly, a voice boomed out over the waves. 'This is the coastguard . . .'

'I think our reward is getting rescued,' Emily laughed. 'We might get a hot chocolate if we're lucky!'

Twenty-one

Lectures and Rewards

Next afternoon Emily was reclining on the sofa in the guest lounge with her foot propped up on a pile of cushions, writing up a full report on Operation Gold (including Operation Map Thief) in her notebook. She'd spent the morning at the hospital having X-rays. Her ankle wasn't broken, it turned out, just badly sprained. Now it was strapped up and the pain was wearing off. At least having to deal with doctors and hospitals had distracted her parents from asking too many questions about how one of their guests had ended up being stranded on a remote island, rescued by the coastguard and arrested for theft and attempted murder. Although Emily had glossed over the whole being-threatened-at-gunpoint episode. For some reason, parents could be a bit funny about things like that – even ones as laid-back as hers.

The Lighthouse was unusually quiet. Mum had gone out to do the food shopping and Dad was upstairs doing battle with some paperwork at his desk. The Hartley family were at the beach and Mr Tanaka had checked out that morning.

When the doorbell rang Drift sprang up from his post at Emily's side. She could tell from his Happy Ears that it was Jack and Scott at the door. 'Let yourselves in!' she called.

'How's the invalid?' Jack asked.

'I'm *not* an invalid!' Emily protested. 'I've only sprained my ankle!'

Jack grinned. 'Great! I was hoping you'd say that. You won't be wanting your present then.' He held up a bag.

'Present?' Emily was so shocked at the notion of the boys bringing her a present she nearly fell off the sofa.

Scott reached into the bag and pulled out a mammoth tub of ice-cream. 'Rocky Road,' he said. 'From Dotty's. But if you don't *want* it, we'd better take it away . . .'

Emily made a grab for the tub. 'Spoons are in the kitchen!'

Scott was running back down the spiral staircase with three spoons and a bowl for Drift when the bell rang again. He opened the door and came face to face with Detective Inspector Hassan.

The size of a grizzly bear in a perfectly tailored old-fashioned cream suit, D. I. Hassan was an imposing presence. He lowered his bulk into an armchair opposite Emily's sofa and regarded the three friends with a stern gaze. Even his spectacular black moustache seemed to be bristling with anger.

Uh-oh, Scott thought. *We're in deep trouble.*

D. I. Hassan pinched the razor-sharp creases above the knees in his trousers to straighten them – even though they looked as if they'd been precision-checked with a ruler already. Then he puffed out his cheeks and sighed. 'Your actions yesterday were *extremely* foolhardy. You could have got yourselves killed. Please leave these matters to appropriate law enforcement officers in future. You must *never* approach an armed man.'

Jack put his hand up. 'Excuse me, Fox *wasn't* armed when we approached him. He was being a total wally, paddling round in circles in a sinking dinghy!'

'And we had no idea that there was going to be a *gun* buried with the gold . . . ' Scott explained. He wanted to point out a few more things – like the fact that they hadn't *approached* Simon Fox when he pointed the gun

159

at them but had run away as fast as their legs could carry them, *faster* than their legs could carry them in Emily's case! And as for 'appropriate law enforcement officers', there hadn't exactly been a whole bunch of them on duty on Gulliver's Island! But somehow he didn't think D. I. Hassan was interested in debating the details of the matter.

'Well, now the lecture is over,' D. I. Hassan's moustache suddenly twitched as he smiled, 'I would like to thank you for helping to catch a devious and ruthless criminal. Interpol has been interested in Sebastian Fargo for years.'

'Sebastian Fargo?' Scott asked, wondering whether the inspector had accidentally skipped ahead to his next meeting. 'Who's he?'

'A man with many identities,' D. I. Hassan said. 'Simon Fox is just one of his aliases!'

Emily's eyes widened. 'Ooh, he's a *smuggler*, isn't he? Is it drugs? No? Weapons? Of course, that's how he knew so much about that old rifle!'

D. I. Hassan shook his head. 'No, not smuggling. Fraud. He hoodwinks elderly people into investing their life savings in his bogus schemes. He promises them enormous profits but, of course, they never see a penny of their money again.'

Emily frowned. 'That's so *mean*!'

'Indeed,' D. I. Hassan agreed. 'His usual MO is to move into an area and befriend one of the local ladies.

He worms his way into her confidence and taps her for all the local information he needs to target people with money to invest.'

Scott laughed. 'Hmm, I wonder who *that* could have been . . .'

D. I. Hassan stroked his moustache as if it were a pet cat. 'Obviously, I'm not at liberty to name names.'

'Of course not,' Emily said, with a grin. 'You're not one for tittle-tattle!'

'Ooh, such a nice young man, that Simon Wolf!' Jack hunched over and placed his hands on his hips in a perfect impression of his arch enemy. 'Does that mean Mrs Loveday will be thrown in prison for being Fox's accomplice?' he asked hopefully.

'Of course not. She didn't know anything about Fox's activities. Not that I'm saying it *was* Mrs Loveday, of course!' D. I. Hassan added hastily. He cleared his throat. 'Anyway, I didn't come to talk about that. I've been asked to present you with these'. He placed his briefcase on his knee and took out a glossy plastic bag.

Scott exchanged doubtful looks with Jack and Emily. What was D. I. Hassan going to give them? Handcuffs? ASBOs?

'We have informed the South African Embassy in London that the stolen Kruger Ponds have been found,' D. I. Hassan said. 'They will try to track down the descendants of the original owners and return the money to them. And some of the gold will be put on display in various museums. But the ambassador has asked that you each be given one of the coins as a reward.' He handed Jack, Emily and Scott a small leather pouch each.

Scott eased open the drawstring and slid out a beautiful gold case containing a gleaming Kruger Pond set on a little cushion of red velvet.

Jack read out the engraving on his presentation box. '*Presented to Jack Carter, in recognition of courage and honesty*.' He grinned. 'Courage and honesty! Yep, that's me to a T!'

'These coins are highly valuable,' D. I. Hassan said. 'Keep them safe!'

'Of course,' Emily said. She would always treasure the coin as a reminder of their adventure on Gulliver's Island.

Jack held up his Kruger Pond. 'I wonder whether it's worth enough for a private plane.'

Scott shot him a look.

'Only joking! Hey, where's Drift's reward? He was the most courageous of us all!'

Hearing his name, Drift pricked up his ears and barked happily. Emily ruffled his fur. 'He can share mine.'

'And there's one more thing,' D. I. Hassan said seriously.

Here it comes, Jack thought, *I knew there'd be a catch!*

The Inspector reached into his briefcase and handed them each an envelope. 'One of the elderly couples who almost invested their life savings in Fox's scam asked that you be given these rewards.'

Scott pulled three brand new fifty-pound notes out of his envelope and smiled. It wasn't going to buy a fast car or a gold-plated palace, but it was more than enough to replace the mobile phone Fox had smashed against the wall.

'I'm going to put mine in my savings account,' Emily said.

Jack slid the notes over each other, enjoying the crackle of the crisp new paper. He'd never held so much cash in his hand. He could think of a million things he could do with this money and none of them had anything to do with bank accounts. First, there'd have to be an enormous chocolate cake, and then another visit to Planet Adventure and . . .

Jack's daydreams were interrupted by D. I. Hassan hoisting himself out of his chair to leave. The Detective Inspector glanced at the tub of Rocky Road melting on the coffee table. 'I can see you've got some important business to attend to, so I'll leave you to it,' he said. As he reached the door he looked back over his shoulder. 'Just *try* to stay away from trouble, eh?'

Emily smiled sweetly. 'We will.'

'At least until we've finished this ice cream,' Jack mumbled, popping a loaded spoon into his mouth as D. I. Hassan closed the door behind him.

Emily dug her spoon into the Rocky Road before Jack

could polish off the entire tub. 'Of course, if trouble comes looking for *us*,' she said, 'what can we do?'

Scott laughed. He had a feeling that, in Castle Key, it wouldn't be long before it did!

Don't miss the next exciting mystery
in the *Adventure Island* series

THE MYSTERY OF THE
MISSING MASTERPIECE

Available now!

Read on for a special preview
of the first chapter.

One

The Great Fête Riot

'*And the first prize goes to Emily Wild and Drift!*'
The crackly PA system could hardly be heard over the roars of the crowd.

Scott and Jack cheered and whistled. In the ring, Emily knelt down and buried her face in her little dog's soft fur.

Drift sat proudly as the mayor pinned a red rosette to his collar. His ears popped up in an expression of

Eager Excitement; the black one pointing at the sky, taking in the applause, the white one with brown spots tucked back towards Emily, in case she had further instructions. He was feeling extraordinarily pleased with himself. They'd just aced the Obedience Trial in the dog show at the Castle Key summer fête for the third year running. And they'd left the competition standing – not to mention sitting, begging and rolling over. Drift trotted round with Emily in a lap of honour, as if he'd won Supreme Champion at Crufts.

Emily high-fived with Scott and Jack as she came out of the show ring. She was pretty stoked with the victory too. The Obedience Trial had been a walkover. Drift could churn out Heel, Stay and Fetch in his sleep. Emily had also taught him a range of commands more suited to an Undercover Agent's Right Hand Dog, of course, such as Stake Out and Lookout Duty.

'Entering Drift in the Obedience Trial is like playing Wayne Rooney in the school under-sevens football team,' Scott laughed. 'No one else stands a chance.'

'Did you see that border collie that kept trying to cut in front and put us off?' Emily asked.

'Yeah,' Jack said. 'We were about to make an official complaint!'

'So what does Drift have up his sleeve next?' Scott asked. 'Brain surgery? Synchronized swimming?'

Emily laughed. 'We're working on this brilliant new command called Distraction. We'll show you when it's ready. Right now, let's find something to drink. Being champions is thirsty work!'

Drift panted in agreement.

'The refreshment tent's over there,' Jack said. 'I just happened to notice they have some pretty awesome cakes.'

Scott rolled his eyes. 'Why am I not surprised?' Jack could detect a single cake crumb, the way sharks could detect a drop of blood in the ocean.

Scott had to admit that this whole village fête experience was turning out to be a lot more fun than he'd expected. He'd only really come to humour Emily – and to cheer Drift on in the dog show, of course. True, the lucky dip, the plant stall and Guess the Name of the Teddy Bear didn't exactly have the thrills and spills of a day out at Alton Towers, and the most extreme ride of the day was a gentle stroll round the green on a donkey, but the fête did have *some* things going for it, like the coconut shy (Scott had won five times) and the sight of Colin Warnock, the curate, dashing around with his video camera. He was taking his filming as seriously as if he were directing a new Star Wars movie.

Inside the marquee in the centre of the green, a long trestle table was crammed with cakes and cookies of every kind. 'We'd better pick three each and share them,' Jack said. 'Or maybe *four* to be on the safe side?'

The friends sat down with drinks and cakes and a bowl of water for Drift. At the next table, an artist had set up an easel and was sketching portraits. Scott recognized Mrs Roberts, their next-door neighbour in Church Lane. At least, she was *Aunt Kate's* next-door neighbour. The boys were staying with their great-aunt for the summer while their dad was away on an archaeological dig in Africa. Scott couldn't help laughing at himself when he realized he was actually starting to think of Stone Cottage as *home.* He'd never have believed *that* could happen when they'd first arrived from London just a few short weeks ago.

Mrs Roberts smiled shyly behind her large glasses and waved to the friends. A small mousy lady with neat, straight black hair in a bun, she didn't fit Scott's image of an artist. Artists should look more, well, *artistic.* More like Emily's mum, for example, who was all floaty kaftans and mad hair pinned up with paintbrushes.

'Mrs Roberts used to be my art teacher when I was at primary school,' Emily explained. 'She's really nice. You know the blonde girl who's helping Vicky White with the donkey rides? That's her daughter, Laura. She's working at the riding stables at Roshendra Farm for the summer.'

Jack snagged a cup from the next table and pretended to peer at the tea leaves. He nudged Emily's elbow and laughed through his mouthful of chocolate cake. 'Ah, yes, what do we have here?' he cackled, doing his best gypsy fortune teller impression. 'Scott will suddenly develop a burning interest in horse-riding!' He reverted to his own voice. 'You can tell by the way he was looking at the lovely Laura. *Ow!*' he added as Scott's trainer made contact with his shin under the table.

Emily had got used to ignoring the boys' scuffles. 'So what are we going to do next?' she asked.

'Let's ask Mrs Roberts to do a picture of Jack,' Scott said. 'Then again,' he added, 'drawing his ugly mug would probably break her paintbrush or something!'

There were more kicks under the table. Emily sighed. The boys were great fun. They were usually brave and sometimes smart, and they could both be pretty useful in a crisis, but neither of them had the ability to plan beyond the next five minutes. 'I didn't mean *now*. I meant, what's our next *investigation* going to be?' It felt like light years since they'd found a treasure map and a chest of hidden gold, even though she was still limping slightly from the sprained ankle she'd picked up on Gulliver's Island. But she was already on the lookout for a new case to solve.

Jack looked around the tent as if a fully-fledged mystery might be hiding behind a tea urn. Since they'd arrived in Castle Key and made friends with Emily, they'd had some awesome adventures. But things *had* gone a bit quiet lately.

'I was talking to Mrs Loveday at the cake table and she told me there was a major kerfuffle in the Vegetable Competition this morning,' Scott suggested. 'We could investigate that. Someone accused Old Bob of bribing the judges to award his onions Best in Show.'

171

'Oooh, *controversial*!' Jack laughed.

'I am *not*,' Emily stated firmly, 'embarking upon an investigation named Operation Onion – however controversial it may be!'

Jack snorted. Coke bubbles spurted out of his nose.

'Well, we can't just order a mystery on the internet,' Scott laughed. 'We'll have to keep our eyes open and be patient.' He grinned at his brother. Emily wasn't exactly known for her patience! Then again, nor was Jack. Scott began to hum *Whatever Will Be, Will Be* just to wind them both up. But he stopped mid-hum as the marquee was suddenly transformed into a tornado of smashing plates, ripping canvas and pounding hooves.

'What?' Scott spluttered, springing out of his chair.

A wild-eyed donkey trailing strings of red, white and blue bunting stampeded past. It was followed by Vicky White and Laura Roberts. '*Wallace! Stop!*' they screamed. But Wallace was in no mood to stop. He buckarooed his way across the tent, scattering tables and chairs and cups and saucers in his path, until he reached Mrs Roberts' easel and head-butted it into the air. Meanwhile, a second braying donkey careened onto the scene, heading straight for the cake table. People fled in every direction. 'The starter gun for the children's sack race spooked them!' Vicky shouted.

'*Gromit! No!*' Laura yelled as the donkey's hooves slammed down on one end of the cake table, flipping the other end up like a giant see-saw.

A barrage of Victoria sponges, chocolate brownies, fairy cakes and flapjacks rained down. Buttercream bombs pelted Mrs Roberts' easel and meringue missiles spattered the vicar's cassock. Glacé cherries and walnuts sprayed the tent like machine-gun fire. Drift was having a lovely time licking whipped cream and strawberry icing off the grass.

Emily nudged Scott and pointed at Colin Warnock. The curate was still filming, in spite of the chocolate sprinkles stuck to his crest of purple hair.

There's nothing mysterious about a pair of crazed donkeys running amok in a cake tent, Scott thought, *but it's certainly livened things up a bit!*

'I'm covered from head to foot in cake!' Jack shouted, throwing out his arms. 'Have I died and gone to heaven?'

THE ADVENTURE CONTINUES

Secret agent tests
•
Character profiles
•
Hidden codes
•
Exclusive blogs
•
Cool downloads

DO YOU HAVE WHAT IT TAKES?

Find out at
www.adventureislandbooks.com

Illustrations © Roy Knipe